Rescued by a Highlander

by

Susan Payne

Rescued by a Highlander

The Wild Rose Press, Inc.
PO Box 708
Adams Basin, NY 14410-0708
Visit us at www.thewildrosepress.com

Publishing History
First Edition, 2020
Trade Paperback ISBN 978-1-5092-3311-3
Digital ISBN 978-1-5092-3312-0

Published in the United States of America

Dedication

To my lovely daughters for the hours of reading and encouragement with which they always supported me. And my husband who still takes my breath away with his sense of romance.

On the ride back to the fortress, Gawain had not turned around, knowing what the young woman looked like up in the saddle. Her legs splayed to both sides of the animal covered with the tight knit hose most men wore while riding through woods, the chainmail covering her more interesting attributes. The short length of dark blond hair emphasized her chin and jaw line which spelt beauty to his eyes. Her mouth, though most often held in a mutinous frown, appeared kissable.

In fact, Gawain wanted to kiss it into a soft poutiness, make those green eyes spark with desire not hatred. Even though he may have to sleep with one eye open to prevent the little vixen from piercing him with his own dagger in the night, he would think the experience of bedding her well worth the danger. He knew a smile settled on his features as he imagined her squirming under him once they were in his bed. Such thoughts had made for an uncomfortable ride home.

SCOTLAND 1754

CHAPTER ONE

Two figures huddled near a smoky fire, dwarfed by the large conifers surrounding them. The dampness those same trees held to the ground was making the silver-haired man shiver uncontrollably. Another day without food, their growling stomachs would be the music they went to sleep with again tonight. The old man was already frail and the single cloak about his shoulders not enough to keep the night cold out although in this thick forest, the sun never seemed to permeate enough to relieve the chill and damp anyway.

The younger, thinner of the two stirred the ashes, trying to ignite the branches, but the damp had done its damage. All it did was disburse what heat was there and cause more smoke to rise in front of the weary travelers. Just as both sets of eyes seemed to close from sheer exhaustion, a noise alerted the youngest they were no longer alone.

"Stand and show yourselves, we have you surrounded," a man's voice shouted close by, too close for those on the ground.

The old man tried lifting his head and make out what was happening, disoriented from his recent tumble into sleep. The thin youth jumped up with sword in hand, stepping between the old man and the much larger intruder welding a wide-bladed sword of his own.

Gawain noted the young man was wearing cheap,

light-weight chainmail which most blades would easily pierce. The helmet, that would have protected his head, still lay on the ground where it had been removed for the night. He judged the man to be no more than sixteen or so with most of his growing yet to do. No muscle filled out his chest or arms. The boy's hair hung straight covering the beardless skin of his face. Gawain was about to say something to disperse the tension that erupted at the first warning call when the youth began a fight in earnest.

The young man raised the sword and swung, trying to drive Gawain away from the fire and the man still on the ground as if planted in place. Unable even to realize that running was his only salvation.

The two swordsmen went at each other as if life were on the line. Gawain first merely wanted to know whom his hunting party had been following and why they were on his property. A hunt for stag became a scouting party when they came across tracks of two horses moving furtively through the forest. Staying to areas with low cover, which in these thick woods was difficult to find.

The ground was barren of all but moss due to the lack of sunlight filtering down through the canopy of leaves and needles. It was the scent of smoke that finally led Gawain and his men to where their prospects were camping so early in the day.

He could tell by the now wide swings of the sword that the younger fighter was tiring from the expense of energy it took to lift the heavy blade. He planned to let the younger man wear himself out so Gawain could claim victory without an unnecessary death.

Gawain had had enough of this. He had lost a day

of hunting to this ridiculous trailing of two weary men who didn't seem to pose a threat to his clan. Renewing his attack, he went at the combatant with his still ample vigor - driving the youth back until a downed tree prevented further retreat.

Just as Gawain was going to knock the sword out of the other's hand, he heard a feminine voice shout out, "No, Father!"

Gawain turned slightly to see the old man had finally revived himself enough to try to lift a sword from the saddle he had been leaning against. The other two burly men of the hunting party grabbed it out of his hand. However, that wasn't what caught Gawain's attention. It was the fact that the yell was not one of a youth, even a sixteen-year-old, but that of a woman.

He looked at the now prostrate swordsman and smiled as he recognized the difference between a half-grown male and a fully-grown female. However, that didn't make Gawain forget the anger and original strength behind the sword swings he had blocked from inflicting tremendous damage to his own body.

Standing over the woman, his sword point at her exposed throat, he asked, "Do you relinquish your weapon and stand to parley?"

The daggers thrown from her green eyes would have made a lesser man rethink the offer, but Gawain merely smiled and said sotto voiced, "You are not stupid enough to think you can escape me and my men." A statement not a question, then finished, "And what of your father? He is too weary to continue even if I were to send you on your way this very instant. We noticed your horses are about worn down to skin and bone, too."

Which was a snide way of telling Jillian she appeared worn and frazzled, she was sure. Well, she didn't care. She wasn't there to appease his sense of chivalry or to look comely for him and his men. If he tried anything like that, she still had the dirk her mother had given her before she died strapped to the inside of her thigh.

Jillian was furious she had allowed these three men to sneak-up on her. She hadn't even been aware she and her father were being followed. She would need to think quickly to save her father from the death she knew her cousin had planned for him. But how to do so under the watch of three large men?

Their horses seemed much fresher than the ones she and her father had been riding for the past two weeks. If she could get two of those mayhaps they had a chance of escape. But how to get her father mounted? It had taken all her strength and a large stump to do so this morning. His strength was dwindling faster than hers without food and water and his health was precarious to begin with.

"Very well, I surrender under duress," Jillian stated as she plunged the sword into the earth and regained her feet without taking her gaze from the man who bested her.

The large man chuckled. "All surrender is under duress, believe me." He pulled the blade from the dirt. "Who are you and why are you on my land without permission?"

The man she fought asked his men to remain beside her father now relieved of his weapon and, it seemed, his will to fight, as well. His frail appearance worried her even more compared to the strong, healthy men standing either side of him.

Righting herself, she stood in front of the leader, not taking for granted he wouldn't stab her through now she was no longer armed. "My father is Lord Riley, Earl of Crawford from the north, and we are simply passing through. Returning to England," she said without introducing herself.

"You travel light for two people going so far this time of year. Is it possible you have not told me the truth and you are, in fact, wanted for some crime? Thievery? Murder? Mayhem?" he asked in a teasing manner.

Jillian wasn't about to find humor in the situation. "As you just pointed out, we are travelling light. Hardly a thief then without a pack horse carrying sacks of stolen treasure."

Still smiling, the dark-haired man with the thick stubble on his face making him seem even more menacing, continued, "I didn't say you were good at it." Then glanced over to her weakened father and asked, "Are you in fact, Lord Riley? That was a grant given as a reward by the English king to families who have done him a service. What service have you done for him that you received such a boon?"

"I married a niece who had been giving his Royal Majesty a difficult time at court over his pestering her older sister. She had turned him away from her sister's bed. It was the farthest property he had available at the time," her father told the man honestly for it was no secret within their family. Jillian took pride in the knowledge her mother had stood her ground when faced with a king's wrath. The good woman was forced to marry a man she came to love fiercely as a penance.

Jillian felt her mother's blood flow through her veins at times such as this. When she was needed to protect those, she loved.

The leader turned toward Jillian again. "So, your mother was a termagant? A type of flea on the monarch's ass to the point she was sentenced to live in the crags of Scotland?"

"My mother loved her home. So, did we, until my father's sister's son decided he had waited long enough for his inheritance. He moved into the castle to take over from my father. Then as Father's health failed, Dennis took over more and more of the duties of the lord. I could see my cousin was not content even then and I needed to take my father to safety. The need to leave quickly and without provisions was one of necessity not poor planning," she threw at him angrily at the assumed derision.

"I was asking for my own curiosity. I take an interest in anyone who tarries on my land, but I can see your father and horses are both in need of rest and good food. I am, Laird Macgregor, and as your host, I will escort you to my keep and give you time to recuperate before carrying on with your trip."

"No," she protested loudly. "I mean, I thank you for your generosity, Laird, but my father must be in England as soon as I can get him there. I do not know if you are the only men following us."

"I saw no signs of anyone else and we were well back when we spotted your trail crossing that of a herd of Red deer we were trailing. But see to your father before you turn down my offer. He does not appear well." The Laird glanced toward her father barely able to stand any longer, grasping the strong arm of one of his captors to stay upright.

"Only for a day, then." Jillian relinquished without gratitude.

"For as long as I say," answered the man in charge as he turned and told his men to saddle the two still tired horses for the lord and his daughter, allowing the old man to sit and rest once again.

"I can saddle my own bloody horses," Jillian said as she stomped toward the animals tethered to a branch nearby.

The Laird waved his men off and let her lift and belt the saddles. Then one of the men helped Lord Riley unto his mount while Jillian got onto her own saddle after tying her helmet to the back. She rode next to her father behind the Laird, who was at lead, with the other two men bringing up the rear as if they were securing criminals or captives of war to the dungeons.

The men all dressed in similar clothes proving they had been out hunting when they came across her and her father. Leather breeches to protect their legs from thorns and brush, wool tunics with long thick sleeves for the same reason. Crossbows were hanging from their saddles as well as a sack probably holding the bolts to use in them. Wide belts held both swords and knives to be used on the game and their boots appeared expensive and of a quality seldom seen this far to the north. The Laird must travel to the south for some finer things. Mayhaps she could convince him it was time to make a trip to the border to stock-up on winter gear. If she could travel with such a man, her cousin wouldn't dare attack them.

Jillian, still feeling raw from her capture, for she could not look upon her so called host's ultimatum as anything besides what it was, rode silently. She and her father were his prisoners. His easily made remark of 'for as long as I say' did not go unnoticed. She did not doubt her ability to escape and hide from any search party he may send out after her. The same could not be said for her father.

Her chest ached as she pictured him swaying with fatigue. He had looked so helpless trying to come to her aid, unable to even lift the sword let alone swing it with any kind of accuracy. Yet he had bravely tried…tried because he could see she was losing her battle with the much larger competitor.

And she had been losing. She did not doubt the other man's strength or stamina. He had more of both than she did. Her female body less able to handle the weight of the sword for more than a few minutes rather than the hours her host could probably maintain.

It was hopefully the last time she would need to face the truth that no matter how long or how desperately she trained, she would not have the strength to fight off an attack by a man the size of the one riding in front of her now.

She felt the horses speed up of their own volition, telling her clearer than any words they must be close to her captor's home. She could see the outline against the horizon, the dark stone defensive wall with a central gatehouse and the higher roof tops of the keep rising above that.

Peering up as they passed through the gate, the murder-hole where boiling oil or burning logs were dropped onto any invaders was easily discerned, even in the dark. She tried not to show the shiver that ran down her spine. Her father's castle was large but this one was more defendable. Even without the now unused moat, crossing the barmkin outside the wall would put anyone in jeopardy of the arrows flying from the bows of the sentries positioned on the ramparts.

How many hundreds of years had this castle stood? How many times had invaders been pushed back and killed trying to unseat the lairds of this land? She knew the history of her father's castle, but it was a history of men who had no link to her. No blood flowed through her veins from those other lords. They had all been extinguished before her father had been granted the title and land of Castle Crawford. She wasn't sure how she felt about riding into the encampment of her host without more knowledge of his loyalties and allegiances.

The horses crossed the inner bailey, their hooves now clapping nosily on the paving bricks uniting the stables and the keep. The wide doors into the living portion were closed in a manner of unwelcome. Jillian peered around the courtyard as if it was her last peek of freedom. She watched as the two other men helped her father from his horse and one of them let her father hold onto him as they walked slowly toward the doors.

Jillian dismounted on her own. She wouldn't allow any sign of feminine weakness impact what would be done with her and was expecting to be treated as an uninvited guest. She felt naked without her sword, but all her weapons beside the dirk had been taken from her and her mount. She stood stoically waiting for orders.

Due to the slowness of his guests' horses, the group did not get back until long after nightfall. The horses were led away by the stable lads and the two huntsmen left to go to their homes as soon as Gawain dismissed them. Once inside the door of the large stone keep, Gawain sent Lord Riley to follow a servant to his room while he led Jillian to one himself.

He could tell she was on edge the entire time they walked down the darkened halls, usually lit by the daylight that made its way through the arrow loops. After a very convoluted route, Gawain stopped in front of a door and bowed her in.

"I will send someone to you in the morning. It is late, but I know there will be food in the kitchen and I can have you a meal if you desire one."

"No, no food." Then added belatedly, "Thank you. I will just sleep and we will be on our way as soon as daylight breaks."

"Are you sure your father is in such danger you would chance killing him in your rush to get to England? He is almost falling down with weariness and lack of sustenance. You will have only a body to deliver back to the Sassenachs if you try to keep up this pace."

"What will you have me do? My cousin is not legally in charge or able to answer to the king, as long as, my father is alive. I have seen his avarice. How he covets everything my parents ever had, even me. He threatened to detain me, rape me, and get a child on me to secure his way to the title," she admitted heatedly.

"So, this isn't just about your father, then. You have a reason for running from home, too." He watched her with narrowed eyes trying to see how much this threat meant to her escaping her cousin.

"I would gladly sacrifice my freedom and my body if it would ensure my father's life, but it wouldn't have. Dennis is more than capable of killing my father once I was his wife. He is too ambitious to be satisfied in waiting for a natural death. Marrying me would be leverage for the king to bestow the title and wealth that goes with it to him. After all, Dennis would not be following the male linage. The King would need to grant the lands and he may have someone else in mind, someone else he needs to keep away from the royal courts."

"Well, there is time to figure out what would be best for your father. For now, I expect you to stay inside this room until morning when I will send someone to you."

"Of course, Laird. Your wish is...." And that was all Gawain heard before the door shut in his face.

He could not keep the smile from forming as he thought about the impudent vixen and turned to continue to his own rooms not far away. He was wondering if he should post a guard. Then realized she didn't know where her father was sleeping and he knew she would not leave without him.

Deciding to keep his dirk nearby as he slid into his bed, he was unsure how the young woman would thank him for her room and board once she was rested. He knew she had a dirk if not more weapons hidden on her person, but he wasn't about to search her physically. He didn't trust himself enough to quit once his hands were on her.

On the ride back to the fortress, Gawain had not turned around, knowing what the young woman looked like up in the saddle. Her legs splayed to both sides of the animal covered with the tight knit hose most men wore while riding through woods, the chainmail covering her more interesting attributes. The short length of dark blond hair emphasized her chin and jaw line which spelt beauty to his eyes. Her mouth, though most often held in a mutinous frown, appeared kissable.

In fact, Gawain wanted to kiss it into a soft poutiness, make those green eyes spark with desire not hatred. Even though he may have to sleep with one eye open to prevent the little vixen from piercing him with his own dagger in the night, he would think the experience of bedding her well worth the danger. He knew a smile settled on his features as he imagined her squirming under him once they were in his bed. Such thoughts had made for an uncomfortable ride home.

She wasn't one who would choose the normal path and her story intrigued him as much as her person. How did a well-born young lady learn to fight like a knight and who let her run around dressed as a male even to go so far as to allow her to cut her hair? Gawain did not fall asleep as readily as usual, his mind and imagination keeping him awake much later than normal.

CHAPTER TWO

Jillian snapped awake at the first sound of someone outside her door. She spent the night trying to rest, yet, listening for any sign the Laird or one of his men was coming for her. She was not so innocent she did not see the interest in her host's eyes or the way his gaze raked her from head to toe whenever he looked at her. Although she wasn't sure he was aware of it, not yet anyway.

She contemplated trying to use that as a means of escape or to convince him to help her make her way to the border. But she didn't actually have womanly wiles which her cousin was prone to point out at every chance he could. Of course, his thinking her as manly and un-natural was what kept him at bay for as long as he had. Now, desperation seemed to be urging him on to take greater and greater chances. She knew her father hadn't wished to order Dennis to leave in case the man took over the castle outrightly. In case Dennis had convinced enough of the castle's inhabitants that Lord Riley was too weak or senile to continue in his position. Dennis had played on their distrust of Jillian, as well. Only the knights and other warriors were loyal to Jillian. Accepted her as one of them and knew her capabilities.

But if her father was shown to be too weak, if she were taken prisoner, if she were forced to submit to her cousin's wishes through needing to protect her father, then the castle could be Dennis's. If – if – if.

Now all of that was mute. Dennis may have control of the castle, but he was there as a guest and not the lord. So much more was needed to become the lord of the castle. To replace her father, and if the king agreed, Jillian as ruler there.

When Dennis decided he had to be closer to her father than a sister's son, her cousin decided he would commit the ultimate sacrifice and marry Jillian. He also admitted he would bring in his mistress as soon as the vows were consummated.

Jillian had punched him in the nose and left him bloody on the floor of the dining hall with a final epitaph of, "Over my dead body," ringing in his ears. That was the day before she took her father and escaped into the night.

A light tap announced the entrance of a young serving girl. She smiled shyly. "I've come to set up your bath for you and to bring you clean clothes. My master said yours have been lost along the way and you have naught, but what you wear." She stared at the clothes Jillian still wore, the tunic and hose as well as the men's styled boots.

"I, ah, yes, I only have these clothes, but I want them cleaned and returned. Did he tell you otherwise?"

"No, m' lady, he din'a say what to do with your soiled clothes, but I can get them back to you by evening. There's a stiff breeze today which should have all dry by then."

"Thank you, then I will leave you in charge of their care. What is your name? I do not like not knowing who people are."

"My name's, Ann, m'lady." And she gave a little curtsy.

"I'm not 'my lady' any longer, Ann. Call me Jillian and we'll get along very well."

Ann seemed worried and confused but answered,

"Yes, m, yes, Jillian. I'll be right back with the hot water and tub."

Several men carried in the tub and then buckets of hot water. Ann provided a towel and bath salts although she peered worriedly at Jillian's cropped hair and tisked. "I can mayhaps bring some pins and we can pin the front bit back, but I don't know…."

"That's all right, Ann. I simply let it dry. I don't do anything special with it."

"Not even to go downstairs? Dress it up for dinner mayhap? There's lots of people at dinner, umm, the Laird and all, you know." Ann tried to convince Jillian of the need to do up her hair in some manner. Suggesting it be woven into braids on the sides or curled in ringlets in the back.

"I – let – it – dry," Jillian said distinctly, but not angrily.

"Yes, m, Jillian. Do you wish me to help you disrobe for your bath now?" Ann asked somewhat cowed by Jillian's refusal to have her hair styled.

"No, I've been bathing myself for years and I find I am completely capable of doing so. I will call when I am done so we can get rid of the water. If you can, will you ask about my father," Jillian said having already taken off the chainmail the night before to get more comfortable. It was lying on the corner floor along with her wide, heavy belt sans the sword.

Settling down into the water, Jillian felt more relaxed than she had previously in this grand home. Her father may have been master of a castle, but that was a dramatic name for what really was more of a reinforced manor house. While the size of what she was in now was overwhelming to her. It being the largest and most fortified of any she had seen before.

Not that she had seen many. She never strayed outside her father's lands since her mother passed over eighteen years ago. Jillian didn't even remember what she had looked like, but sometimes when she smelled verbena, she remembers a woman coming into her room and singing to her. Jillian had tried to remember those songs, but cannot hold a tune. She thinks if the woman was her mother then Jillian had not inherited her fine singing voice.

Jillian pulled the dress on to cover the lace trimmed smock before putting her arms into the quilted short gown, tying the lacings on the front tightly to her thin frame. The shoes didn't fit, being too long, but they stayed on her feet if she walked with care.

Ann returned with a braided cord. "I think we can tie this around your waist, my, Jillian, and it will hold the pieces in place. The gown might be a little short. You are a fine tall female, that's for sure. I don't think I've seen such muscles on a woman before."

As Ann thought about her honesty, added quickly, "Not that they're not feminine or anything. Simply that most of us never get that kind of exercise, except mayhaps the washer woman." Then her eyes got large again thinking Jillian may take offense and find the comment rude.

Jillian smiled instead. "I spent a lot of time working on these muscles, Ann. Lifting logs and buckets of water so I could finally be able to swing a full-sized sword with accuracy. I still practice weekly, but haven't recently. I've been traveling."

As Ann picked up the corset Jillian had discarded from the clothes, Jillian said, "I never wear stays. I do not need them and it hampers my movements too much. You can take them back to where you got them."

Ann nodded without saying anything and took the offending stays after cleaning up around the tub.

Then remembering again, Jillian asked, "Have you heard anything of my father?"

"Oh, yes. He was up early and ate a large meal then asked to return to bed which is where he is right now." Ann answered as she picked up the pile of dirty men's clothing and took them out the door with her. "Someone will be back to take you down to the hall although most have already eaten and off for the day."

Jillian would like to be able to tell Ann she didn't need food, but that would be a lie and would be more detrimental to herself than anyone else. She needed to build up her stores of energy as well as get her body rested. Continuing to take her father to England was their only salvation. Once there, they would need to beg old friends for the favor of food and lodging. She didn't know what else she could do. Petitioning the king and proving her father could not keep his property protected wasn't going to gain support of their wish for the king's help.

The door opened abruptly and a rather formidable woman a few years older than Jillian entered without ceremony. This was not a servant. Her clothes were of very fine quality and a gold necklace proclaimed her to be a lady of the household. She wore a lace trimmed cap and white apron over a round dress. Certainly not the master's mother so mayhap a wife? She was definitely someone who found Jillian's presence a bother and unnecessary interruption to her life.

"I've been told to bring you to the hall for a meal.

Everyone else has been fed, but the servants will bring you food." Then she turned quickly. Jillian stepped swiftly and with her longer stride caught up with the shorter woman, but did not ask anything of her.

Jillian wanted to tell her that if Jillian had had her way, she and her father would both be gone from this place and miles away by now. But this woman wasn't the object of her displeasure and waited until she saw that gentleman to make her complaints known.

Instead, she bit her tongue and followed the woman through the passageways and down two sets of steps before finally coming out into the open. She saw several long wooden tables and benches in a great hall boasting a large fireplace at both ends with sizable fires wafting heat throughout the room.

Jillian sat where the woman indicated at the end of one of the first trestle tables, near the fire and furthest from the head table. Jillian did not take it as a slight. After all, she had tried to kill the master of this house. She wasn't here on her own decision. More as a prisoner, but for now she would have to accept it. Once she got her strength and sword back, it would be a different matter. Once her father was stronger and rested, as well. Then they would be on their way, hopefully, without her cousin finding them and putting an end to their one chance at freedom.

Another older woman entered the hall wearing a large apron and a kerchief over her head. She brought a large bowl of brose and a hunk of soft cheese on a piece of brown bread. A cup of cider also appeared in front of Jillian and her stomach growled noisily knowing it was so close to having something inside it for a change.

Giving a quick thanks to God, she began eating.

She was unable to keep herself from gulping the hot toasted oat mixture down by the spoonfuls and taking bites of bread and cheese in between. She finally slowed as her stomach decided it had enough or too much. Jillian spent a few minutes without adding anything to her body, letting the food catch up with her before losing it all after eating so quickly. She finished her meal at a more sedate pace and felt better as it stayed down. She would not make that mistake again. It wasn't a pleasant way to spend her time.

The woman who guided her to the hall finally came back. "It is time for you to return to your room. I'm busy and cannot take the time to watch you."

Jillian, her normal confrontational-self present, answered, "I can stay down here until my father shows himself and then get ready to leave. I can find my way back to my room for my things."

The woman gave what could only be described as a venomous glare. "Those were not my instructions. I'm to leave you in your room to rest."

Jillian knew whose orders those were and was about to argue, then realized she wasn't ready to leave, yet, anyway. She needed to make sure her father was rested and stronger and that they could get to their horses. Retrieving her sword was another worry for another time.

It wasn't until the evening meal was being called that the well-dressed woman again arrived unannounced at the bedroom door and demanded Jillian follow her to the great hall. Jillian did as she was told since she was hoping to speak with her father. She was sure he would be there at this time of day. She hoped he would be more rested and they could now plan to leave on the morrow.

As they entered the hall, Jillian went toward the table and bench she had occupied that morning, but the other woman continued walking past it. On towards the raised head-table before stopping and turning with a sour face to Jillian. Pointing her to the chair next to the larger central chair, Jillian stared into the eyes of the man who engaged much of her thoughts that day. First with curiosity and then with anger, flipping between the two until she thought she would go mad with it.

Drawing her brows down in concern, she realized her father sat on the other side of the Laird, the expression on her host's face inscrutable. She did note that he too cleaned-up well although even yesterday in the murky light of the forest, he looked good.

His sharp blue eyes watched as she stepped onto the dais while she noticed the shoulder length black hair brushed back from his face, showing off the now strong clean-shaven jaw and cleft chin. She assumed there could be slight dimples framing his wide lips, but he wasn't smiling at the moment so Jillian was on guard as to his intentions.

He wore dinner dress extremely well. Broad shoulders filled out the wool cloth coat and lace hung to mid-hand, brass buttons decorated the front and wide cuffs. A brocade waistcoat with wide lapels and lace cravat covered what was left of his shirt. His buff colored breeches tucked into high boots as he stood waiting.

He raised one eyebrow to indicate his uncertainty to her mood.

"I won't stab you with my eating knife, Laird, so you have no worry. I see my father is content and stronger and I have you to thank for that."

"I merely gave him the time he needed to sleep and some food. He did the rest. I see you are much more…" He stopped to let his eyes rove over her body and back to her face. "Refreshed and rested yourself."

"I am and I thank you, but I must implore you to return my sword and allow my father and me to leave and be on our way," she said prettily. She wasn't used to using feminine wiles to get her way but wasn't averse to doing so if they worked.

Her host took a deep breath. "About that, I believe your father and I came up with a plan that would safeguard his life and make the long harsh trip to England unnecessary." He glanced away a moment before meeting her gaze once again, but not before she saw the pupils enlarge and focus on her lips.

Her father was too far away to speak with, but he turned toward his daughter and smiled. More relaxed than she had seen him for months, ever since her cousin had invaded their home and began to take over. Jillian relaxed, too, seeing how calm her father was and sat back getting ready to enjoy her meal.

The dishes were brought out to the table by servants who eventually sat at the end of the long trestles and kept jumping up when a bowl was emptied or something more was needed. The service appeared effortless and as long as Jillian could ignore the many curious glares and outright stares, she enjoyed the food placed in front of her.

Gawain found himself unable to take his gaze from his female guest for more than a moment and tried to keep his mind on the present, not on what he would like to do with her later in the night. He recognized her beauty yesterday once she allowed him to know she was female, even with her damp hair looking like muddy seaweed hanging down over her face. Now, it was a brilliant red-gold and framed her face in rippling tendrils. Her large expressive green eyes still sent him daggers, but they were sheathed more than on the previous afternoon.

Her mouth was often the object of his attention as she took small pieces of meat and vegetables daintily between them and chewed slowly, letting her tiny pink tongue sneak out and sweep any juice from the moist lips and then disappear again. He found himself almost hypnotized by every little movement and he couldn't understand why.

He was uneasy as to her reaction to her father's decision. What he had seen of her temperament did not bode well for an alliance, but something deep inside him knew it was what he wanted, what he desired. It would be an interesting next few days. After that, he hoped his patience and stamina would be rewarded. Whether Jillian ever agreed would be the foremost question and would be left unanswered for a while, yet.

Jillian had been surprised when a round wooden trencher was brought for her and the Laird to share but since no one else noted it, she accepted the food as he placed it in the trencher and pushed it towards her. Finally, unable to eat another bite she smiled and shook her head so the Laird ate the last pieces of meat he had selected for her. He emptied his cup and asked for all the cups to be refilled.

The servants jumped up from their seats and went about the tables filling the cups and mugs again as the clan turned toward their Laird knowing something special was about to be announced.

The Laird stood and raised his cup, then proceeded to say loudly, "Clan Macgregor, I formally introduce you to my guests, Lord Riley, and his lovely daughter, Lady Jillian."

The clan, to every man and woman, except for the woman who had been Jillian's guide, raised their cups in salute. Jillian nodded her acknowledgement as did her father but did not raise their cups.

The clan's leader continued, "After this very short acquaintanceship with Lord Riley, I have found a kindred heart in our love for Scotland, our distrust of the English King, and our esteem for his daughter."   .

This last made Jillian almost gape in disbelief. But he wasn't done with the surprises.

"I have the great honor to announce that Lord Riley has given me permission to wed his daughter and become a part of his family as he becomes a part of ours."

At the announcement, a great amount of foot stomping and cups banging the table-boards ensued as the loyal clan wished their Laird and his soon to-be-bride well. Jillian, on the other hand, looked to her father to await his rebuke of such a calamitous claim. When he would not meet her gaze, she glared furiously at the man beside her knowing he was the instigator of such a momentous mistake. She wasn't any man's wife material. She wasn't even thought of as a woman by most men she was acquainted with.

Jillian went to stand and leave the dais when the Laird grabbed her hand preventing her removal from the table saying loudly, "And as is tradition when a clergy is not available, I handfast Jillian and we will wed when the spring and the priest return."

This last was met with roaring cat-calls from the men and blushes from the women as they tried to prevent their men from sending some of the more risqué messages of encouragement and directions for their leader. As Jillian tried to find a route of escape, she noticed the chair of her guide was empty and the food on her plate left half-eaten.

Trying again to pull away, the Laird pushed his chair back with his legs and followed her off the dais. Retaining hold of her hand and then arm, he steered her toward the stairs and the passageways off it. Jillian mutinously stomped more than walked beside him as he guided her toward her room, only he didn't stop there. They continued further on to another door Jillian was loath to enter. He pulled her into the room with him and then Jillian thought, closed the door with a sigh of relief.

She turned towards him, demanding, "What was that about? What have you told my father that he would think this was a good idea? I wish to speak with him, alone, privately, right now."

The Laird turned the key in the lock, evidently to lock her in rather than to keep others out. "Your father and I had a long talk this afternoon and we decided this would be the best for both of you."

"You decided! You decided? Why would you decide anything about me and why would my father ever agree with a complete stranger? I don't even know your name other than you're the Laird of Clan Macgregor and that I don't like your sister or whoever that is you put in charge of guarding me."

"No one is guarding you and you probably are

referring to my cousin, Agatha, who has made her home here since my mother died several years ago," he said banally.

"I don't care who or what her name is. I was merely stating facts. That I know nothing about you and surely cannot be expected to marry you in the spring or at any other time."

"Gawain," he said.

"What?" Jillian asked confused by the single word.

"My name. It is Gawain Macgregor and I'm the Laird and have been for over five years now. The clan voted me in and I have every means to remain Laird. You will be Lady Macgregor and our children will all have the last name of Macgregor."

She could only stare dumbfounded. The man wasn't rational if he thought there could be any kind of relationship between them. What could have put such a thought into either of their minds? Men. Always thinking they had the answers and must tell the little, weak female how to go on. She wouldn't let this stand.

"I need to speak with my father and explain how bad a plan this is. How impossible this marriage is. You don't even know me and I can tell you – we will not suit. I am not a wife for anyone. Least of all you."

"Your father and I don't think it that bad of an idea at all. We spoke for a length of time and have come to an agreement for both your sakes."

She should have searched her father out this morning no matter what anyone else said. She should have gone to him and made him understand that only the king could protect them from Dennis and his mad plans. She should have never stopped off in those damp woods or lost the battle with this impossible man.

"No, there has been some mistake. My father would never have agreed to this without even talking it over with me. No, no, this is not like him at all and I'm worried he isn't himself. That this trip as done something to his mind." She was becoming worried as she thought the only possible answer was that her father was ill in his head.

"I assure you, the man I spoke with was perfectly rational and made rational decisions for his life and your safety." He gazed into her eyes to decide if she were sensible enough to speak with. "Are you ready to listen to me?"

Jillian folded her arms across her chest. "Alright, I am listening." But the movement merely lifted the round firm breasts up, causing the swells to show above the neckline of her dress. Gawain was finding it difficult to keep staring into her eyes and not let his gaze drop to the cleavage that was just out of his line of vision. But he must make this stubborn woman listen to reason. Not only for what he wanted, but for her own life and that of her father.

"Your father was very distraught this morning when I found him. He realized how dangerous and perilous your position. That if it had been your cousin's men who had come upon your camp instead of me, the outcome would have been much different. Instead of sleeping in a warm clean bed, he felt he would be in a shallow grave along the road. And you would be taken and abused and held captive for the rest of your life, even if your cousin cut it short."

When Gawain was sure he had her attention, he continued, "I offered my home and my protection to both of you and he assumed I meant marriage. I thought about it and found that I would offer for you. This way, he will remain safe with the strength of my clan behind him and you will be away and above your cousin's reach as my wife."

Gawain wasn't sure she believed it was that simple so he added, "I think you fighting me, the chance you could have been killed in front of his eyes made your father realize he could not protect you during an attack. Or from his own nephew if that man and his men continue pursuing you. After hearing your father's account of what happened these last few months, I believe he is right."

"But I do not need protecting, he does. I am nothing, a pawn mayhap, but if my father lives, he is still Lord Riley. As long as he lives, only the King can take that away from him."

"You would be a pawn that would be used to control your father and you must know it. With our marriage, your father is welcome to stay here indefinitely and you will be safe from anyone trying to control him through you."

"I would not allow myself to be used against my father," she stated emphatically.

"You wouldn't be able to stop it. Do you think even your death would relieve your father of his feelings of guilt or grief? Think about this rationally. Your father is tired and old and worried he will die and leave you in a precarious position. Now he has all those worries put to rest. I will protect you, protect him if need be, and your cousin will be impotent against him with the King."

"What happens now? I'm not familiar with this custom other than when our own people couldn't make it to a church for a wedding. Is it different for a Laird?" Jillian was familiar with big pompous weddings of clan leaders, especially when one clan joined forces with another and people travelled for days to attend and celebrate. She would have time to make other plans before something like that could be planned and completed.

"We go on as if we had been in front of a priest. We are legally bound and they, the clan, are expecting me to bed you and show them proof of our consummation. Nothing too rigorous I assure you, especially not for a woman such as yourself willing to die for her father. I assume you knew that would have been the outcome of our combat yesterday if I had continued to battle with you. This is much less arduous I assure you." He smiled at his own joke.

"I won't do it. You will have to force me, if you think you can." She pulled the dirk from under her skirt and held it toward him, threatening him if he were to come nearer.

"I knew you had some sort of protection to make you so adamant you could keep me at bay." Reaching for the blade, he sliced his thumb before she could prevent his hand from making contact.

Gawain took his bloody thumb and made a smear on the sheets. "That should be good enough for the show. I'm no expert but it can't be worse than that, can it?"

They both stared down at his handiwork. Neither made a comment for a moment as they contemplated the stained sheet.

"I, I don't know. You did that for me? So, I, so we...," Jillian tried to explain how she felt about his using deception with the clan to save her from going through with the consummation.

"This should be only between the two of us. I think it a disgusting habit that should be done away with, but for some reason it is still expected that women remain 'pure' to be considered proper wife material. I will still need to remain here, for at least part of the night to make it seem normal."

Jillian glanced around the neat room with the large bed beneath the intricate wall tapestry and several chests along the wall. "But it's your room. I should go back to mine," she argued feeling she owed him something for his consideration.

"To the household, this is your room now, too. My parents and theirs before them never kept separate chambers. It is a tradition I agree with. That way, a married couple has some time privately together to vent or yell or whatever needs to be done to clear the air each night."

"It sounds like you know more about this marriage business than I," she confessed watching as he continued removing his clothing.

"I had good examples. Now get to bed. The morning will be here before we know it." He waited as she removed the outer gowns and shoes before walking over to blow out the candles. "I sleep naked and I don't want any complaints about it."

CHAPTER THREE

When he turned back to the bed, he could see his wife laying where the blood smear was with her feet flat on the mattress and her legs splayed, the skirt of her smock pulled up to her waist exposing her female delights to his eyes with only the moonlight shining through the uncovered window.

"What are you doing now? You look like a sacrificial lamb," he told her as he moved closer, drawn by her body as if metal to a magnet.

"I don't wish to be the reason for you needing to lie to your people, your clan. As you say, it can't be worse than a prick to the thumb, can it? Besides, if I give myself to you, then it is one more reason for my cousin not to want me to wife. Even if we are not married, I will no longer be a maiden in truth," she said as she explained her thinking, but remained staring up at the ceiling. "I am ready," she finished stoically.

Gawain's body reacted as any mans would given the same opportunity. He searched for reasons to remain celibate. Give her time to get to know him, give her time to be used to being married, and give her time to come to accept her destiny. Although she seemed to have decided to set her own fate, laying there waiting for him to consummate their union.

He reminded himself he had originally planned on bedding Jillian this night. At least his body had planned on bedding her. He had to admit he knew he could not force her to accept him as her husband and had thought he may be sleeping alone, as he was used to doing.

He never brought a woman to the keep. What few

women he had taken his satisfaction with were experienced women and widows who decided they missed the arms of a man. He never promised them anything more and always left a substantial amount to placate them in the morning when he was gone.

But this was different. She was there offering herself to him. Even giving him rational reasons to continue to the conclusion. She would be further out of her cousin's reach and she was willingly laying there in calm acceptance. He stepped closer and tried to decide what his answer to her request should be.

She saw his well-formed backside before he extinguished the candle. His arousal or lack of it was out of her line of vision. She was afraid to move enough to catch sight of it in case the size made her change her mind. The men she practiced against often went almost naked in the heat of summer when the exercise of swinging the massive swords and pikes caused their bodies to sweat profusely.

She had overheard their teasing of one another, too, and knew that the part of their anatomy that differed the most from hers grew to unfathomable size. It was used to pierce and fill women's bodies in a myriad of ways. Many of which Jillian felt must surely have been impossible and merely men bragging to one another rather than being true. It was simply that the same stories would surface time and again that made her doubt her disbelief.

Gawain, although his manhood had been reacting vigorously to the sight in front of him said, "Well, I'm not."

In the moon light, he could see Jillian lower her brows in confusion as she said, "I thought men were always ready. I mean, I know you do not go around with a man's yard, umm, arousal, but I thought that if an opportunity presented itself, that it was involuntary."

"What do you know of men's arousals? What maid knows of such things?" he asked wondering just what kind of a life his wife led before coming here.

"I spent most of my time in the stable and bailey where the men practiced fighting and sword play. I started as most squires, taking care of the equipment and then working with wooden swords and shields against the quintain. I had to work on my strength before I could work with the equipment. That is why my arms and legs are so muscular and firm. Not soft like a woman is."

"I find nothing unfeminine about your body. Even with strength, you could not be confused with a male." Then he reminded himself of their fight in the woods and his mistaking her for a lad. "Not when you aren't covered from head to foot in male attire and chainmail, anyway." He was next to the bed and he let his hand stroke her bare arm.

The feel of her skin, soft yet firm under his fingers and the scent of her this close as she lay there open to him, the pink of her womanhood showing through the strawberry blond curls was working against his decision to leave his wife her maidenhead that evening.

He found himself asking, "You've thought this path out then? You wish us to continue as the rest of the clan expects us to?"

"I find that it makes the most sense for both of us. It is not as if I ever wish to marry so no man will miss what you have taken."

"Am I taking or are you giving?"

Again, those brows drawn down in thought. "Is there a difference? I am willing to lay with you and, yes, give myself to you. Is there something more I should be doing?"

Gawain lowered himself to the bed and stretched out alongside her. He realized how well they would fit together, his hips and hers almost aligned and he could still easily kiss her as they made love. But not tonight, tonight he did not want her to feel trapped or feel he was taking advantage of her offer.

"Why do you have your knees bent like that?"

"I walked in on a couple in a barn and this is how she was laying. Is it wrong?" she asked innocently.

"Not wrong exactly, but I think if you relax and lay flat, you'll be more comfortable. We will worry about variety once we are more experienced with each other." He stroked the bare arm closest to him and he could tell she was nervous and held her body stiffly. He felt what control he had slip away, leaving him wanting this woman as he had never wanted another.

Unsure why she held such appeal, such draw, he decided he would become her husband even if she were not ready to become his wife.

"Relax. I'll not do anything without telling you first. I merely wish to calm you. If you change your mind about this we will go back to our original plan. Does that sound right to you?" he asked quietly, almost a whisper as he leaned toward her ear.

Jillian nodded but did not release the tightness in her muscles. Gawain felt her tenseness beside him.

Gawain continued to stroke the other arm saying, "You have silky skin, smooth and pleasant to touch. I enjoy doing this with you, laying here, and feeling how soft you are compared to me."

As soon as she relaxed to his touch, he stroked her bared leg until she accepted his touch there and let out a sigh as trust replaced suspicion. He let his fingers slide across the soft skin of her thigh, still bared and open to him. She tensed as he touched the soft curls on her Venus mon. She took in a deep breath and expelled it as she closed her eyes and let him continue with his exploration.

Wanting to cover her mouth with his as he reached her most private part, he thought she would find it invasive, even more so than his intimate touch. Kissing was so personal and he did not feel she was ready to accept him in that way, yet. But as a sexual partner…. He did expect her to accept him in that manner, as long as he did not show too much desire or ask her to respond to his actions.

His finger slid into the silky warmth and felt her become moist immediately in response to his touch, which almost undid all his good intentions as he kept from groaning in need. He let his fingers slide further and enter her deeper, getting her used to feeling him there inside her if only with his hand.

The previously hidden nub at the top of her channel began to firm and grow as he rubbed it carefully with a slight pressure. He kept whispering soft encouraging words as she began to breathe in short pants and he felt her internal muscles clasp his finger as she unconsciously squeezed him.

A few minutes of attention and Jillian was thrashing her head back and forth on the mattress, her hands grasping the sheet in wads as she fought the sensations welling inside her.

"Let yourself go, Jillian. Relax and let it happen. Trust me, I'm right here, let it come."

Jillian didn't seem to understand what he was saying, but responded by relaxing. Then she was in a wild whirl of emotion and feelings as she clutched him to her body during the throes of passion he elicited. As she was trying to catch her breath, Gawain placed his erection at the same entrance that had just given her such pleasure.

"If I enter you now, I think it will be the least painful."

Jillian nodded in agreement. Gawain stopped his penetration when he came to a barrier, waiting until she was aware what was happening and not still reacting to her orgasm. Jillian must have felt him hesitate and pushed her hips up into his, settling him to the hilt and he stilled once again as he was sheathed in her moist warmth.

He rested his forehead on hers. Unable to go slowly any longer, Gawain set a pace that soon had him stiffening - his neck stretched taught, arms rigid as he held his weight off her. Grinding his hips deeply until the last spasm left his body, he laid to her side to catch his breath. Keeping his arm across her body, he could monitor her emotions by feel.

Jillian was still analyzing her own physical response to Gawain's touch and then had to figure out what actually happened to him. Was it the same for both of them? He seemed to respond differently in a way, but the increase of his heartbeats, his breathing, and the following lethargy seemed to mimic what she discovered happening to her own body.

And the pain was minimal. She hardly noticed

since she was so overwhelmed with her own rapture as well as feeling Gawain's body as it entered her, stroked her body internally. She wondered if she hadn't just lived through that mind shattering euphoria, would his penetration have caused it as well? Was that what all the talk and innuendos were about? All the things the men stopped saying when they realized she was near enough to hear them?

Living as a woman in a man's world opened her up to hearing, seeing things proper young ladies would not have access to, but she had no one to ask so had to live with part of a truth she was sure. If she had a mother or female relative, she would have had someone to ask, but her father kept a male household. Even her tutors had been men.

Men vetted thoroughly by her father, young men who knew not to compromise their student in any fashion. Young men who spent a lot of time visiting with some of the other men in the crofts.

Now, after this experience, she was sure she would remember conversations cut short or expressions curtailed when she came nearer. Her father's men may have been older, but they were men and used to living roughly. Soldiers who lately had no battles.

She was unsure whether she could walk among them now and not realize the undercurrents. Not that they lusted after her since she was treated much as their daughters would have been if they had stumbled into the training arena. But now she knew much more about things personal. Things a husband and wife have between them. These past few minutes had altered her life as she knew it and as she would forever know it.

Her husband had added much to her knowledge

and she felt more a woman than at any other time in her life.

Gawain finally pulled himself back to reality after experiencing the strongest orgasm of his life, even without Jillian doing anything exotic. But when she raised her body to meet his, when she in fact forced his penetration, he lost all sense of reason. Only the need to bury himself into her body controlled his every motion and finding release in filling her with his spend. Something he had always been careful to prevent with any woman before Jillian. But he didn't want to think of those others. Jillian was the most wondrous woman he had ever come across.

"Now we are truly husband and wife. Now no one will be able to force you from here, from me," he told her as he let himself sleep next to Jillian as she, also, fell into deep, relaxed sleep.

Gawain was almost fully dressed when Jillian woke. Standing near the washstand as he strapped on his sword belt and dirk, he turned to her as she walked towards him. He smiled then said, "You should make sure to keep your hair worn down like yesterday. I marked you last night when I lost control," he said as he reached toward her neck to see the love bite just under her left ear.

He hadn't realized he had done so at the time. He knew he wanted to join with her, but resisted covering her mouth with his and thrusting his tongue into her as he thrust his erection. Instead, he found his mouth sucking the soft skin behind her ear on her neck, and he must have done so with passion because the bruise was readily obvious. Not that he cared if the whole clan knew, but he did not want anyone to say something that would embarrass Jillian, not until she was more comfortable making love with him.

Then it wouldn't matter if she had love bites or she scratched his back as she spiraled out of control. The thought of his making love with her again had parts of his body jerking to attention and he had to pretend to be occupied with getting his belts in place.

Jillian pulled back from his reach saying, "I always wear it down like that. I don't waste my time braiding and playing with my hair all morning."

Gawain dropped his hand at her maneuver away from him and continued to finish the buckling of his belts. "I am going back out to finish the hunt that was interrupted. The kitchen is calling for more meat and my men and I rarely disappoint." Then he turned to leave.

"When will Agatha come for me? I wish to speak with my father."

"You are my wife. You have access to any room in the keep as well as the bailey," he told her.

"But what am I supposed to do?"

"Ask Agatha. I'm sure there are things she would be happy to pass along to you as lady of the house. She is always complaining about how busy she is running this place so now you can divide it between the two of you." He left her staring in the mirror at herself.

Ann came in right after Gawain left, as if she was outside waiting for his leaving as her cue to enter and help Jillian with her dressing. She carried a set of women's clean underclothes and blue sacque dress asking, "Should I bring up the tub again, Madam?" When she saw the expression on Jillian's face continued, "I don't feel I can call you anything but

Madam now you are the Laird's wife." She hesitated again and finished, "You'll still be Jillian when we're alone then, m, Jillian, if that's all right."

"Call me what you will. I do not wish a bath. I'm anxious to speak with my father. I didn't really get time yesterday and I am worried about him." However, she did not explain why she was worried, that after his complacency of last night she wasn't sure he wasn't more ill than he let on.

Once Jillian was dressed, Ann grabbed the stained sheet and wadded it into a ball saying, "I've been told to bring this to Agatha. She will be in charge of it."

Jillian shook her head in disbelief, but was too interested in finding her father to argue on where her soiled sheets got taken. She hurried along the way to the hall where she knew she would find most of the people awake in the keep. She was correct, seeing her father sitting and talking with a lovely older woman, her upswept gray hair covered with a cap and two braids left to hang alongside her surprisingly smooth face.

"Father, you appear so much better. I was worried you were getting weaker," she said as she approached the two, both with empty plates in front of them.

"Ah, Jillian. Daughter, I would introduce you to, Lady Edith. She is the healer of this keep and I am feeling so much better since following her advice," he told his daughter while accepting her kiss on his cheek. His eyes seemed clear and he was freshly shaven with his hair pulled into the usual queue at the back of his neck. She could see this rest was what he needed.

"Lady Edith, I have you to thank for my father's increased good health, then?" she asked and stated. The woman's smile was warm and genuine. She wore a dark blue short gown over a lighter blue round dress with lace sleeves and white lace trimmed cap over her once golden hair. Her father didn't stop staring at the woman as if he couldn't get enough of her beauty.

"Well, you had already done the best thing for him by removing him from your home. After examining his nails and hair, I am certain he was being slowly poisoned. Being away from that danger helped him survive and now with a few herbs and lots of water, I do not see why he won't be with us for many more years." The woman gazed into the old man's eyes then lowered her own in shyness.

Jillian took into consideration what the woman said, then nodded. "That is when Father began to get weaker and have problems regaining his strength. I thought it was due to Dennis' constant browbeating and demands for more control of the property and cattle. I had no idea he would resort to actually trying to kill my father in so insidious a way." Jillian stroked the silver-white hair on the head that was so dear to her.

"I will let the kitchen know you wish food and let you two speak privately. Lord Riley has been worried about you and it will impede his convalescence to have so many items on his mind. He needs to rest all of his body including his brain before he will heal and be the man he was meant to be, even at this age," Lady Edith teased as she left the two alone.

Her father appeared worried. "Are you very angry at me for handfasting you to Gawain without consulting you? I was still so weak and I was afraid I would not be able to protect you from your cousin any longer. It made sense to align you with a strong warrior. I think you will get along if you give him a chance." He looked up at her, concern coloring his watery eyes.

Jillian could no longer stand in censure or give him the reprimands that had been building up in her. Ever since she woke to find herself the wife of a stranger and her body given in sacrifice to pay for their sanctuary, she felt at peace.

She was not sure Gawain wouldn't have allowed them to stay with him until they both grew stronger, but it was too late now unless Jillian left him before they stood in front of a clergy and said their vows.

Handfasting could be broken, especially if both parties agreed, even after a consummation. Jillian was hoping she could convince her father to return to their original plan. Leave Scotland to seek help from someone strongly related to the King.

"Gawain seems like a nice enough man, Father, but that was not our plan. I still feel we can make it to England, especially now, once we are stronger. And the horses can carry us further in a day if we can take a few extra provisions than what we had when we left home."

He gazed at her sadly, saying, "But Daughter, we had no destination and England is a big place. Most of my friends are old and if they even remembered me, would not feel an obligation to take us into their home or speak to the King to favor my cause. It was a wild plan and, I thought, the only choice available to us."

Spreading his hand wide, he encompassed the high ceiling and large beams of the hall, the two huge fireplaces and glass windows. "Now we have a home right here where there are kind people and plenty of food and good care for both of us. Your husband seemed very concerned you had not had enough food lately and that you had taken on too dangerous and difficult a task to get me to England. Now you won't have to, the need is gone."

Staring deeply into her father's eyes, she tried to see if he was diminishing his own wants and needs thinking it was the easiest and best thing for her. She didn't want her needs to be considered in this decision. Losing his land and title to an upstart spoiled brat, dangerous though he was, should not be so easily contemplated.

She wanted him to fight, she wanted to fight and after learning about the poison, she had no objections now of running her cousin through with her own sword.

Some of her thoughts must have shown on her face because her father said, "Daughter, think about the title. In Scotland, the law doesn't prohibit titles from following the female line if the King does not place any ruling against such a thing occurring. Even if Dennis had some way of making that happen, of getting the King's favor, if you begot a son while I was still living that boy could be my heir. He would be much closer in blood than a sister's son, a nephew, a son of a man with his own family name and legacy."

Jillian had not thought that far ahead. She was more of a day to day planner with the ability to change direction quickly if needed. She thought about her child inheriting, for her to be the mother of the Earl of Crawford. She could see that happening and she could live in the castle until he was of age to care for his title and lands. When he reached his majority. The idea was far from an anathema to her.

Lady Edith came in followed by a servant carrying a tray laden with food and cider, a pot of tea as well as toasted bread with melted cheese on top. Jillian turned and attacked the food as she usually did every other morning at home before going out and working with the horses and practicing and training with the men who guarded the castle.

She was trying to find a way to do the same here and not embarrass the men or anger Gawain. A husband in a bad mood wasn't someone she could control even if he was besotted with her…and Gawain was far from besotted.

During dinner, Jillian wasn't exactly warm towards him, but she shared the trencher and complimented both the game bird and venison he and the hunting band brought back. Then she thanked him for offering her his wine and asked to be excused from the table to get ready for bed.

Gawain was surprised by the request, but thought possibly the conversation with her father earlier in the day had her understand she was safer here with Gawain than on the road to England. He stayed a while longer so it did not seem as if he was rushing after her and left when his cup was again emptied.

Opening the door to his room, he expected to find her in one of the chairs but instead she was already on the bed in somewhat the same pose as the night before only covered by the sheet.

"Are you trying to tell me something, wife?"

"I thought this is what I was supposed to do, be acquiescent and oblige my husband with my body as he wishes. Isn't that what is expected of me?" she asked innocently, too innocently.

Gawain began removing his dinner clothes. "That may be what most husbands would expect, but I did not expect such wifely diligence from you. Is there perhaps a dirk waiting for me under that sheet, too?"

"No, I wouldn't need to hide a weapon if I wanted to kill you. I would take you on as a warrior, not like some weakling."

"Then to what do I owe this unexpected welcome?" he asked as he gazed over at her, his chest bare and only his breeches left to remove before he blew out the candles.

"Something my father said. Something I believe you and he discussed when you offered to handfast me. That our child would be his heir if he were conceived before my father died. Now that he is so much better, that could be a possibility. I could have a child and then Dennis would be completely out of the contest. He would have no chance at the title or property."

"So, you wish my seed to make this happen?" he asked casually seeing a possible way of getting what he wanted out of this marriage, too.

"That's how it works, isn't it? I mean you did not seem to mind last night and I will not turn you away."

He decided to use his wife's wants to get what he sought. "I understand you wish me to get you with child. You and I agree that doing so would be very pleasant for me, but I want more."

"More? What do you mean more?" She seemed perplexed.

"I mean that waiting here in bed, ready for me is a good start, but I wish this to be between you and me. Not only to conceive although I have nothing against a child being the outcome of our more intimate endeavors." He stared into his wife's confused face and continued as he kneeled onto the bed. "I want to make love with you. That includes kissing and touching and tasting you, all of you and for you to do the same to me."

"I don't understand. Didn't we do that last night? I mean, didn't I do it, right?"

"Last night was a good beginning. Especially for the two of us coming together as strangers, but you will need to let me guide you. I promise it will not be onerous and I will never hurt you. Simply lay back and enjoy as you did last night and mayhap reciprocate as the urge takes you." He pushed his breeches down, pushing them off with his foot leaving them on the floor next to the bed.

Jillian's eyes were huge watching him prowl closer like a large, dark cat getting ready to pounce on a mouse sitting paralyzed in fright.

He laughed. "Let me show you. The first lesson I should have taught you if I had understood how untutored you were sooner."

Placing his hands on both sides of her face, he gently covered her mouth with his, gently sucking and returning for more before licking his tongue out against her lips and urging her to open for its entrance. She understood his request and gave a soft moan as his tongue entered her warmth and then tried to follow his out with her own. He sucked her tongue into his mouth and reciprocated with a louder moan of desire, holding himself back from moving too quickly now his pupil was showing willingness for his tutelage.

Jillian seemed focused on her mouth and his tongue and his sucking on her bottom lip as he returned again for more of her, bringing her breathing to short pants between kisses. He found he needed to feel even closer and covered one soft orb with his hand, feeling the nipple harden into his palm. Then he left her lips to cover the other breast with his seeking mouth, rolling the nipple with his talented tongue and bringing it to a peak to be suckled deeply.

He did not disappoint. He brushed over the soft hair-covered mound and continued on to the next breast with his mouth leaving the first glistening with moisture that cooled in the night air causing the rigid peak to ache with want. Gawain stopped thinking about lessons and followed his own wants and needs, not understanding his desire to get closer, become more than her lover and instructor, become her very reason for taking breath.

Jillian stiffened as his warm breath blew across her most private part as he leaned over her prone body. He slid his wet tongue between her nether lips and stroked the budding pearl to greater degrees. This was new to Gawain, he had never spent this kind of time with a woman, never wanted to, but Jillian was different. He wanted her to be so besotted with him and with lovemaking she would never think of leaving him, of going to England, of returning to her father's home.

Gawain nestled his body between her legs, letting them hang over his shoulders as he reached up with both hands to fondle her breasts. He rolled the erect nipples between his thumbs and forefingers before paying more homage to the delights he found between her legs.

His wife's breathing became labored and she covered his hands over her breasts and stroked his arms, pulling his head closer to her as he felt then tasted her arousal, first salty and turning sweet as she began to move her hips in contrast to his mouth.

He smiled and gave one last kiss upon her cunny before getting to his knees, leaning in, and penetrating the moist passage he had been honoring. She pulled his hips to her, circling his buttocks with her ankles, holding him as if she feared he would leave her like this, hot and in need of release.

Gawain would never, could never...not even if he had been trying to punish her. He was too far into passionate desire, too far into Jillian to give her up now. He pumped into her with controlled passion until he felt her muscles grasp hungrily at his manhood and then milk it dry as he allowed himself the luxury of calling out his ecstasy.

Collapsing to the side of his wife, Gawain's last rational thought was that he was no longer sure who had been the teacher and who the pupil during those last few moments of lovemaking.

Jillian couldn't believe the incredible sensations her husband could elicit from her body. The body she thought so average, less than average if she compared it to other young women her own age. She was thin and flat chested, or at least all the men she held combat with had told her. That she lacked the curves that made other women interesting and desirable. Yet, here was a man who seemed to enjoy her body, flat chest and all.

His licking and then suckling her modest sized breasts drove all other thoughts from her mind. The tug on her nipples reverberated through her body making her yearn for his touch between her legs as he had the night before. She had been unsure how to ease that deep ache.

Once he placed his mouth over her private female

part, she wanted to climb right onto him. She couldn't get close enough to him and desired that same release she experienced the night before when he brought her to completion. That almost unfathomable feeling of tightening that exploded into a release of sparkling light and sensation of flying.

Jillian spent her time feeling and enjoying and trying to memorize all the various things her husband had done to her. She felt herself blush merely remembering what he did and how much she enjoyed him doing it. She never heard of some of those, or at least if she had she had not understood the act as spoken. The men in the bailey became used to her being there and often forgot she was not only a woman, but the daughter of their lord as well.

Now she had a better idea of what occurred between a man and a woman although she also thought she should have been doing more. She should not merely have enjoyed her husband's attentions although he didn't seem to act as if she had not fulfilled her duties.

Jillian would do more next time. She was curious about her husband's body and his response to having her near him in bed. She found the whole lovemaking act one of great interest. She was beginning to understand why the men in the bailey focused so much of their talk and attention on it. If she had known what a pleasant past time it was, she might have chosen some muscular knight and had her way with him sooner.

She giggled silently knowing she would not have done any such thing. The men were not available to her in that way and they would have driven out any man who even thought to bed her. She spoke the truth when she said they were comrades in arms even though the men acknowledged she was female. They had never restrained themselves when they fought with her in hand-to-hand combat. Knowing at some time she might come up against an enemy who would not hold back, she needed to be ready to protect herself.

But for now, she had a man she had access to and the right to study and investigate her own sexuality as well as his. She finally snuggled down to sleep as her husband was doing. She had time to become more familiar with him before she left.

Jillian quickly pulled her hand back when her husband's eye, the only one showing with his face buried in a pillow, snapped open followed swiftly by a smile as he seemingly remembered the evening before.

"I'm sorry I didn't mean to wake you. I was just touching your ear - it's so, so perfect. The right size and smooth and...," she told him as she returned gently to rub a finger over the sensitive shell shaped skin.

"I don't believe that for a moment. You became bored waiting for me to awaken so you thought you would investigate my body parts. Actually, if you're interested, there are a lot of my parts that would more than welcome your investigation." He rolled onto his side exposing an already rigid staff.

Jillian flushed but did not stop herself from reaching toward him and with gentle, tentative strokes traced his erection. From soft velvety tip to the more massive girth where it joined to his body, near the curl covered sac that seemed to undulate with each touch of her hand.

She followed a vein down and around and another back up the side, watching so intently she almost missed her husband biting the inside of his cheek to keep from moaning and frightening her away from her interest.

"You said I was to learn from you. That I should touch you as you touch me. Does that include tasting you?" she asked not looking into his eyes, but seriously studying his aroused body part.

"I think that would be best left for a different time. I'm most vulnerable in the morning to touch and most often wake wanting a woman. That seems to be something more we have in common, our timing seems to be very much in tune with one another's. That isn't always the case and I think it just one more reason for you to stay with me."

Jillian's gaze jumped abruptly to meet his. How did he know she had been thinking about leaving him? Leaving this house, his clan and taking her father now he was getting stronger. Going somewhere else so they could fight Dennis's attempt to steal her heritage, her children's heritage.

"I'm not planning on leaving here. I have no way of defeating Dennis, yet, if my father will not ask for help from the King," she told him honestly, no longer interested in his body or its reaction to her touch.

He seemed to know the game was over as well. "I know, that's why you asked about getting a child, but you may have conceived already and I am pointing out we are very compatible. I would hate to have to chase you across Scotland simply to retrieve my wife."

Jillian dropped her hand, but that hadn't dissuaded Gawain from a morning lovemaking session, not after having been stroked to almost breaking point. He pushed her onto her back and entered her without any further comments. She shoved her hips up to meet his and he grunted with contentment as he became completely sheathed within her warmth. Then began his thrusts in earnest, reaching his pinnacle quickly, Jillian right with him, proving once again they were more than compatible in bed. If Jillian weren't already with child, it wouldn't take too much time before she was.

Gawain got up and slapped his wife on her bottom in play, saying, "Stay abed, as a reward. I must go and meet with some crofters who live farthest from the keep."

"I could go with you. I'm not used to being so lazy and my horse will need exercising if nothing more." She sat up naked on the mattress, hope evident on her face.

"I have made plans to go out with Sir Jason and Sir Torrey." He named the two men who were on the hunt with him. Both about the same age as Gawain and all three physically fit so she assumed they practiced as well as rode to the hunt together.

"Find Agatha and she should make time to show you around the keep, introduce you to the servants. Cook said she is the only one to meet you and that was when she brought you food to break your fast."

"Yes, and I met Lady Edith, and Ann. I'm not totally without knowledge," she sounded defensive without meaning to. It wasn't her fault Agatha was staying as far from Jillian as she could get. As if hiding from her for some unknown reason.

Gawain left, having other things on his mind. Jillian waited and was not disappointed when Ann came in with a clean underdress and some gossip, which seemed to be what the girl thrived on. Letting little tidbits slip out as she tried once more to convince Jillian to change her hair. Jillian let the talk float around her as she dressed and left Ann to pick up after Gawain.

CHAPTER FOUR

No one was in the hall and Jillian decided to miss the meal and go in search of her father. She should have made more of an effort to find his room yesterday, but to be honest with herself, she had been distracted. Knowing Agatha could show up at any time, Jillian had not thought about making arrangements to speak with him again. One of the things her husband told her was to familiarize herself with his home and she would. If along the way, she found her father's chambers then all the better.

Climbing the main stairs to the top floor, she began her reconnaissance. Finding most of the doors closed, it did not take too long before she was done on that floor not wishing to walk into a private chamber. Besides, she knew her father wasn't on the floor since he separated from her before she was taken to the floor with her husband's bed chambers on it.

She did find a room which contained shelves filled with books and ledgers, a large partner style desk with an open knee-hole on both sides for two people to use at a time. There were various glass ink jars as well as nibs on the desktop. She didn't investigate this room further at this time and would ask Gawain before she borrowed any of the books.

The last floor up from the hall and public rooms of the keep was the most active. But again, most of the doors were closed. Those that were open were sleeping chambers but nothing to indicate whose, no sign of her father anywhere. Jillian decided to go to the basement area, passing through the kitchens and the laundry that opened out to the bailey.

She heard murmuring indicating one of the rooms along the passage was occupied. She was surprised when she ran into her father as well as Lady Edith. Her father appeared to be happy to see her and stood for her kiss then sat back down turning toward the older lady who was using a pestle to crunch seeds in the bottom of a stone cup.

Jillian was glad to see her father look so much better and dressed in a fine coat with several gold buttons down the front and on the wide cuffs. The shirt beneath immaculate with a lace cravat and sleeves. The breeches were loose but of expensive material. His hair was pulled back in a black ribbon at the base of his neck. Over all, he appeared as he had months ago before they rode from their home.

"I need to make a poultice for the butcher," Lady Edith explained to Jillian. "A boar cut his leg as he was going to slaughter it and now the wound has festered. He should have come to me sooner, but men rarely want to admit they are in pain or in need of a woman's help. Once this is done, things should get better quickly. I warned him next time he ignored something like this he could lose his leg." She was speaking to no one in particular, simply venting in female exasperation.

"Well, I am glad you noticed my father's symptoms and could help him regain his strength. I saw him getting weaker and weaker, but did not realize it was due to my cousin more than his attack on our home." She reached over to pat her father's hand, which appeared less frail already.

Her father added. "Now that we think about it, bringing his own guard and even squires would have been normal, but he brought household servants, as well as, cooks. That should have made us more uncomfortable." He shook his head at his own naïveté.

"You are not to take the blame for this, Father. Dennis came as a familiar visitor even though we had not seen him for over ten years. Why would we question his motives? He never appeared to covet your property before. I never would have contemplated that he felt himself worthy enough to claim himself as your heir, not with me there and you still vigorous with life."

Jillian smiled and continued, "But we may win our home back. It will take a little planning, but I realized Dennis is in a much worse position now than when we were still in our castle. After all, unless he has the ear of the King, he has nothing else."

"Daughter, I want you to confer with your husband before you make any plans. He has some ideas of how to remove Dennis without causing a war between those who support him and those who still support me. I do not wish us to jeopardize our future by acting impulsively now."

Jillian knew he was trying not to offend her knowing what she gave up for them to remain in Gawain's home. The surprise of Gawain already being handfasted with Jillian was only one of the surprises the two men planned to throw Dennis' plans off, she was sure. To have her husband's strength behind them when Dennis comes for them is a God-send. And Lord Riley seemed sure Dennis would come for them.

Lady Edith, trying to defuse what she comprehended was a sore point festering between the child and parent, asked, "Have you seen the dungeons then, Jillian? They are not used for prisoners any longer, but they are interesting if you like old cellars. This keep goes back several hundred years and used to have a moat as well."

Jillian welcomed the distraction. She hated being at odds with her father. It had been the two of them for so many years, she wasn't sure if she could add another's voice into the mix before settling on a plan. Gawain did not even know Castle Crawford. How could he have good ideas on how to protect it and win it back for her father? She smiled and told the couple she would take a tour of the dungeons, after all, and went the direction Lady Edith pointed out.

A large key hanging on the wall as she approached the steps heralded the private entrance to the unused portion of the labyrinth. She went down the two steps to stand in front of the sturdy wooden door, large iron hinges holding it up with a leather strap as an opener. She lit the candle sitting there with her flint before opening the door.

Leaving it open allowed some light from the high windows in the passageway to shine across the rough stonewalls and well-worn steps leading even further into the earth. Jillian noticed the lowering of temperature after a few yards into the dungeon and just as she thought she had seen enough, the door crashed closed and she heard the key turn in the lock.

Spinning quickly, she caused the candle to extinguish. She thought she could go directly to the door and bang on it loudly enough to draw the attention of whoever shut the door, probably thinking it had been left open in error. Her thumping did not retrieve anyone to unlock the door, but did make Jillian's hand hurt. She would have hit it with her boot but since being there, she only wore house shoes, which were soft like slippers without a hard heel to make any kind of noise.

"Damnation!" Jillian said as she tried to find the flint in her pocket again and hold the candle at the same time. It was a little difficult until she put the candle in her mouth and soon, she had light again. It wasn't much help for her in her quest to escape. She would eventually be missed, but probably not until supper. By then her father or Lady Edith might remember mentioning the dungeon and Jillian saying she would search it out. Until then she could see how comfortable she could make herself.

As she walked past the old metal cages, many with the doors removed, Jillian realized what the area was used for now. She could see there were casks of wine and oil and other stored provisions, using the natural coolness of the underground sanctum to preserve these items.

She placed the candle on a drop of wax to keep it in place and tried by smell to find something edible. After several tries, she found only the wine and several small kegs of hard cider. Pulling the cork from the wine, she searched the area for something to use as a cup.

There was a large wooden scoop on top of one of the grain barrels and filled that with the red wine. Keeping it on an angle enabled her to drink without spilling a drop while waiting until someone came to find her. The fact that this had once been a working dungeon, Jillian figured there wouldn't be any trap doors or ways out besides the large plank door, which was now securely locked.

The only problem was she wasn't the only living

thing down there. Jillian noticed and smelled the old drain system where excrement had been moved out of the cells by way of shallow open half-pipes made of stone. These once carried soiled water out, probably to the moat area. But now rats and other rodents came up through these openings of the walls and into the storage area where they feasted on whatever dropped on the floor or they could chew through. Jillian noticed that most items were stored in covered barrels and not left in the open to entice even more four legged visitors to the dungeon.

Spotting one just outside the circle of light made by the candle, Jillian wished she had her bow and arrows. Not that it was unheard of to eat rats, but she didn't think she would be down there long enough to find out. She missed the feel of the tautness of the string between her fingers and the burn of her arm muscles after sending several arrows toward a moving target quickly, one right after another.

Jillian stamped her foot, not that the rat paid any attention since the soft slipper-like shoes she wore around the keep evidently were not frightening. She banged down her empty scoop and the rat scurried into the darkness where she heard it make little squeaking noises, or there was something more in there with her. She went with the thought there were many others enjoying the dungeon with her.

She filled the scoop again and wondered if the wine in the other casks was sweeter. She tended to like wine that was more fruity than dry. She investigated her selection.

Jillian had gone through all the poems she knew from memory and thought about creating one of her own, but they all sounded like the drinking songs and limericks the guards hummed and told after returning from town. Some of the words she understood, others she understood more now she was a married woman. Other's still escaped her so it must have to do with things men kept to themselves.

Anyway, she filled the scoop once again and gave the now sputtering candle a withering glare. It too was going to leave her alone in the dark, just as she was pretty sure the original rat had returned with his family members. But there was nothing she could do about it.

Jillian found a couple of barrels to move together to sit on and keep her feet and skirts up off the ground. After a search for leftover lanterns or candles from previous human visitors proved unsatisfactory, she was facing the fact she would be there in the dark soon. Not that darkness bothered her. She preferred the dark because it forced one to listen closer and listening, she felt, was less veiled, making secreting items and people impossible.

Refilling the scoop one last time thinking it would be daunting to do so without light. She sat back down as the candle sputtered into nothing and blackness surrounded her.

Then the scurrying of little clawed feet began in earnest, but they seemed to be staying away from her. Mayhap she should have made a pile of grain to the other side of the room where they would busy themselves until it had all been eaten or stashed away. Now was a poor time to think of that. If they stayed on their side and she remained up on the barrels everyone could live peacefully together. If not, she hadn't learned how to wring a bird's neck for nothing. What was good for the goose…and all that.

Jillian was about to try to make-up a poem when she heard the door scraping across the stone floor and then Gawain calling out for her. "Jillian, are you down there? Jillian?"

Preparing herself for the teasing she would probably receive for getting closed into the dungeon, she called out in reply, "Yes, I'm here. Just give me a moment to get the stiffness out of my legs. I can see where you are from the light behind you."

Gawain took her arm and pulled her to him. Leaning down, he asked, "Are you hurt?"

Jillian pulled her arm away, not wanting to have people think that a little time in the dark would un-nerve her or drive her away. She realized the key hadn't been in the lock where she left it so she asked to be sure, "The key was hanging on the hook on the wall?"

One word from her husband in a controlled voice. "Yes."

There were several people in the kitchen as they came through besides the ones who had been with Gawain, at least two servants following them now.

Gawain said, "We'll eat our meal and then talk."

"I'm not hungry. I would rather go to your room if that is all right with you, husband," she said politely.

"As you wish, I'll be up soon." Whether a warning or a concerned promise, Jillian wasn't sure nor did she care.

Once upstairs Ann arrived immediately. "Oh, Madam, we were so worried. The Laird had everyone out searching for you, even the cook staff who were trying to keep the supper from burning down. How did you get locked in the dungeon? What were you even doing down there? I never go near the place since they say it has ghosts." The last was imparted to Jillian in a whisper.

"Well, I didn't find any ghosts and if they were there, I think they would have come out to speak with me since there certainly isn't much else to do," Jillian said facetiously.

"Can I bring you a bath, then, Madam?" Evidently being locked into the dungeon for most of the day raised her elevation so that she could no longer be referred to as Jillian, but must accept the more formal 'Madam' again.

Even though supper was going on in the hall, there were still servants available to carry the big oval wooden tub and the many buckets of hot water, then cold to cool it down to a temperature Jillian liked. She began to undress and unable to think with Ann standing to the side, sent the girl down to her supper.

"There's no need to hover, Ann. Nothing happened to me and as I told you before, I can bathe myself. Now leave and I don't wish to see you till the morning." Then Jillian, naked, stepped into the tub and slid down so the warm water covered most of her body and she lay there absorbing the heat into her very cold bones. Nothing bad actually did happen to her, but sitting down in the damp and cold brought on a chill to her body she was having a difficult time getting rid of.

She heard the door open and she was about to tell Ann what she would do to her once she got out of the bath, but was too lethargic to even open her eyes.

That is when a very different voice said, "You seem so comfortable in there I hate to disturb you, but I wish to hear what you think happened down there today. I understand the last people who said they spoke with you were your father and Lady Edith. Did anyone else speak with you? Do you know what happened in the dungeon?"

"Someone who is not happy with my being here locked me in as I was looking over the keep as you suggested," she told him wearily, not caring if he knew someone under his roof was less than pleased with his choice of bride.

"I suggested you have Agatha guide you around the keep. It is very large and has been added to over time so some of the rooms are not straight forward. They come off dead end passageways and up back stairs," he told her unnecessarily.

"Those I navigated without error and I would not have gotten locked in if someone had not set-out to do so. I am sorry I made everyone miss their supper. You should have simply waited to search for me. I was fine."

Her husband said keeping restraint on his temper, "But we didn't know that. Your father was sure you would not leave him, not without at least trying to get him to go with you."

"So, that is what this inquisition is about? You thought I ran off and that would make you appear foolish." She was irritated that her bath had been disturbed and the pleasant buzzing sound in her head was clearing. Snuggling down into the water again, she ignored Gawain as he removed most of his outer clothes.

Gawain saw his wife in the still clear water since she hadn't soaped the cloth. It still lay dry on the stool next to the tub. He brushed his hands over her exposed breasts and she smiled saying, "I know I'm not very feminine there. I have always been thin everywhere. The men said I looked like I had two fried eggs under my shirt."

He once more needed to rethink his idea of what his wife's life was like before she came to him. "You are more than enough for a handful. All I need to be satisfied and the bairns will take care of your becoming bigger," he teased as the nipples responded to his touch.

Jillian merely smiled, and continued allowing the water to almost cover her.

"Come up here and look me in the eyes," he said as he leaned towards her, staring intently. "Mad wi it! You're right blootered and smell of wine from here. What did you do down there or need I ask? Found my good wine and whiskey, I suppose?"

Jillian tried to keep her eyes open, but soon closed them due to the bright candle light and said righteously, "I consu-u-umed no whiskey."

Walking over to the towel, Gawain said, "Only because you didn't find it in the dark. Here, stand up if you can and I'll dry you off."

Jillian tried twice before she could get purchase on both sides of the tub to push herself up and practically fell into her husband's waiting arms.

He wrapped the drying cloth around her. "If you think I'll play the gentleman and not take advantage of your being foxed then you don't know me very well." He chuckled as she squirmed within the cocoon as he rubbed her body dry.

Jillian again gave him a big owl stare and giggled and that's when his resolve to treat her gently was lost. He picked her up and carried her to the bed. Unrolling her naked body from the towel, he followed her onto the mattress. She reached out to pull him to her still damp body and he pulled the covers over them so she wouldn't feel chilled.

Gawain liked this wife. She was reciprocating his every move, she initiated kisses. Kisses to his lips, his chin, his eyelids and his chest. She licked his nipples until he thought he would cry-out with want. Then she would not stop rubbing and stroking his bare chest, shoulders and headed for the waist of his knit hose, which he quickly disposed of by kicking them out onto the floor.

They made love finally when Jillian forced it upon him, pushing him down onto his back as he laughed at her attempts to swing her leg over his body and straddle him. He finally became frustrated himself and helped her. Placing his erection at her entrance while she did the rest. Setting the pace and depth which seemed to be too shallow for her needs. He accommodated her as best he could, finding his release as soon as he felt her tighten around him and she threw her head back, arching her spine backwards as the spasms racked her thin body.

Jillian collapsed onto his chest and Gawain held her there until he slid her to his side before curving around her body, marveling at the wildcat he had in his bed. If she let just a little of that out at a time, he would be more than satisfied with his loving wife. And he would have less fear she would one day walk away without a word to anyone.

CHAPTER FIVE

When daylight hit the room, Jillian winced and put up her hand to cover her eyes. The disturbance woke her sleeping husband who hugged her body as he remained curved around her in protection and asked, "Got a head this morning, I take it?"

"Just a wee headache. I don't usually drink much wine and never that much or in the middle of the day," she said slowly and quietly.

"You were down there for hours. I'm impressed you could walk on your own to our room let alone not drown in the tub."

Jillian quietly moaned in pain. "Can you simply leave me in peace for a while this morning. It should go away, I'm sure, with a little quiet."

Gawain kissed her neck, just below the ear, which he found so delightful on their wedding night. "I can leave you alone, but parts of me are still excited about the hellion I slept with last night and want a second go."

Jillian was silent as she thought about what he said and then asked, "So I didn't dream all of that?"

"Nor did I," he said as he nudged his aroused manhood into her back and then lifted her leg to accommodate his body better.

Jillian arched her back, willing to oblige his need as long as he didn't interrupt her peace too much. Gawain seemed to have understood the tacit agreement and pushed into her while fingering one breast and then the nub that grew more interested with each thrust. Jillian leaned her head back while Gawain sucked the soft skin beneath her ear again and nipped her shoulder until she came to a shudder and he stiffened in reaction.

Gawain waited a few moments and then disengaged himself and left Jillian to rest some more. Even Ann did not come into the room until Jillian herself opened the door to let the girl know she could empty the tub.

Cook seemed surprised to see Jillian in the kitchens and tried to wipe the wrinkles from her apron as she approached. "Missus, what can I be gettin' afore ye?"

"Just some bread and cheese if there is any about. I missed both my supper and breaking my fast, it seems," she said as she glanced about the tables and counters in search of food.

"Ahh, I've got better than that, Missus. I just took out some bannocks and we can find a dab of preserves and ye will feel like a new woman." The rotund woman looked to see if Jillian was going to reprimand her for being too familiar.

"I can't say the old one is too perky right now so mayhap a new me is what is needed." She accepted the warm bannock already dripping with butter.

A cup of warm milk direct from the cow was placed beside her as she stood next to the table eating and she drank it down thirstily. "It seems as if I haven't eaten in days."

"Weel, Missus, I almost thought you dinna like me cooking ye were at table so little." She looked pointedly at Jillian's slim hips and backside. "Ye do be needin' a little meat on those bones. I know the young bucks likes to see the skinny malinky long legs, but a woman needs more cushion. Something to fall back on especially if'n she's plannin' on having bairns soon."

Jillian choked on the bannock and then waved it

into the air in salute as she went in search of her next goal. She wasn't about to have a conversation with the cook about children. She still wished to conceive, but that would be kept private between her and her husband. Although it seemed they were both doing pretty much all they could to have her conveniently with child within a short period of time.

It took a couple of tries, but soon she had cornered her 'guide', Agatha, in one of the upstairs rooms that was being turned out. Agatha was overseeing the servants as they moved furniture about the room to clean under it. Jillian caught Agatha's gaze, but the older woman lowered hers to the floor quickly, trying to hide her displeasure at having Jillian interrupt her day's activities.

"Agatha, may I speak with you please." Just as Jillian thought the woman would actually have the audacity to ignore her request, Agatha threw down the dusting cloth and followed Jillian back into the passageway.

"I have chores that must be done today. I do not expect you to understand how much work it takes to maintain a house of this size running smoothly so the Laird doesn't have all those little things bother him when he comes home to rest," she said in a speech that almost sounded practiced.

"I know what it takes to run a house this size. I was in charge of my father's castle after my mother died." Which was true, but not exactly. Their long-time housekeeper continued to run the home and kitchens so Jillian was free to practice with the guards and men out in the bailey most of the days.

Agatha's color was high and she seemed to be

holding back on what she really wanted to voice. Jillian encouraged the other woman to have her say. "Go ahead and tell me what is sticking in your craw. I know it was you who locked that door on me yesterday."

Instead of trying to deny that she had done the deed, Agatha asked, "Does Gawain know, then?"

"Not from me, but he isn't stupid, either. He will figure out who doesn't wish me around and my being here makes little difference to anyone save you," Jillian pointed out.

"I don't care if you know. You are not a proper wife for the Laird or for a knight. I heard that you were found and brought here wearing men's clothing, your legs encased in knit, and riding astride. It's indecent is what it is. Tradition means much to the clan and you are not traditional in any way." Agatha finished emphatically.

Jillian had no arguments with Agatha's remarks. After all they weren't completely off the mark when all is said and done. "Speaking of traditions, I wish to thank you for not hanging my sheets after the wedding night."

Agatha blushed again, a crimson that spread from her neck to her hairline. "I, ah, I was surprised there was proof of you being chaste, but I had asked that Ann bring it to me because I thought there would be no sign of purity upon it. I owe you an apology for thinking you were less than you should be as a bride," the woman said begrudgingly.

"I fight as a warrior because I am my father's only child and we needed someone to lead if we were ever attacked again. It was an area I found more interesting then learning how to do needlework or weaving. And I am much better at it then most men. I simply need to balance out the fact I do not have enough body strength to go into combat against a man without some sort of edge, like surprise and speed."

Agatha stared at Jillian as if she were a strange insect that had invaded the house. "You like to fight? To wear men's clothing and swing a sword?" Her expression turned into one of amazement as she finished, "I heard you raised a sword against Gawain, but I thought that must have been a falsehood since no man has ever bested Gawain."

"I didn't best him either. He took pity on me and realized I was in a weakened condition after having been on the road with my father for weeks. I know my limits and I would never be able to beat Gawain without his having some sort of handicap," Jillian said honestly knowing her own capabilities. She had bested men bigger than she, but Gawain had strength and agility and the ability to react to his opponent's attacks and change in battle technique.

"You are an unnatural woman," was all Agatha could say. Evidently the worse thing for Jillian to be, for Gawain's wife to be.

"I agree I am nonconforming to your description of a woman, but I assure you Gawain finds me woman enough for him," Jillian threw back, tired of hearing this woman denigrate her and her choices.

Agatha was almost beside herself with that comment. Jillian thought perhaps she had gone too far and the older woman would have a seizure of some sort trying to come up with a rejoinder that would knock Jillian down to the level Agatha thought she should be.

"Do not worry. Gawain and I have an

understanding, but I am not sure we make for a good marriage. Why don't we leave things as they have always been? You remain in charge of the house as you have been since you moved here and I will not interfere. If I have a need that is not being met, I will come to you and ask that you see that it gets done. Is that a proposition you can live with?" Jillian dared the woman to refuse the olive branch because if Jillian became angry, she could take Agatha's position away from her. Gawain had already shown he did not regard Agatha as important, not as important as his wife was, that was for certain.

Agatha nodded in agreement. Jillian knew the woman didn't trust herself to say anything aloud, didn't trust she would be able to stop at a mere agreement without fuming about Jillian's unfitness for being the Laird's wife.

Jillian turned towards her room. There wasn't anything of interest in the house and she seemed to put people on edge whenever she came upon them unannounced while they worked. All but Ann, who simply nodded and curtsied and then scurried away. Jillian wasn't used to that and could not imagine what story was being passed around to encourage that type of reaction to her presence.

As she was heading back to her sleeping chambers, the open door to the room with the desk beckoned. She veered towards it like a bee to a flower. She perused the shelf of books with elaborately decorated spines where she found titles like *The Odyssey* and *Don Quixote*. Neither had she read. When she picked the first up, she found it written in the original Greek and Jillian replaced it carefully on the shelf disappointedly. She could read English, Gaelic, and French, but had never been taught Greek or Latin as a male would have been.

She continued and was pleasantly surprised to find an almost new *Le Morte de Arthur* by Castiglione, the story of King Arthur and his court in French. She would ask if she could read that. It had been years since she last read it as a young girl. It was probably one reason she became so infatuated with anything that had to do with knighthood and fighting with the heavy swords, wearing chainmail and helmets, drawn towards destriers and tilting with pikes.

Jillian smiled remembering how her teacher and bane of her existence, Sir Gunn, had worked her harder than any of the others saying she had to work longer and with more diligence because of being a female. No reason was good enough for not doing her best and for not getting more accurate with her weapons. She worked at becoming stronger. Worked out with the various wood logs and bags of grain she carried up and down the loft's stairs.

But all the pushing and threatening made her a better fighter and better leader. The men began to admire her unfailing energy to keep going no matter how weary or how much pain she was feeling. And she did suffer pain, in silence as all the men were expected to carry their own pain. Being a female didn't give her license to rest longer or stop earlier.

A call and the ever-familiar sound of one sword striking another brought her attention to the outside bailey. Two men of equally large proportions were shirtless and fighting one another, the one who was a little shorter than the other being the better swordsman, at least today.

She watched avidly. Not because she was interested in the half-clothed men herself, but because she missed the excitement of such activity. She knew she had lost much of her strength, which she must recoup if she were ever to try to raise a sword in her arm again. She could go back to the dungeon and lift the smaller casks until her arm muscles built-up to their normal strength as she had done as a girl. No one would know she was there and the weighty objects were already in place.

She sensed him before he spoke. "Interested in watching my men practice or simply enjoying watching half-naked men sweat?"

She glanced over her shoulder to give him a little smile. "Mayhaps a little of both. Since we have been together, I don't look at men in the same way. I always appreciated the fact they were strong physically, but I looked at their muscular structure from a combatant's position. Now I appreciate some of the more interesting facts, the hind-quarters for instance. They are not enlarged merely to be able to hold their position against an onslaught, but they are thrusting muscles, too. Their hard areas are in juxtaposed to a female's soft areas."

Gawain came up behind her, pushing her up against the window frame and said into her ear, "You sound like you've been contemplating my men over-much. Haven't I kept you occupied enough?"

"You've been more than entertaining, my lord, but a woman has a lot of spare time in which to think about things." She sent the words out as a challenge, letting him know that a bored wife could get into trouble.

He was ruching up her dress in one hand while trying to free his aroused staff with the other. Keeping her in place with his firm body, his head behind her neck so he could again suck on the soft skin there. Jillian arched into his hips, allowing him the access he was seeking. A low groan as he entered her showed his appreciation and the matching moan emitted from her lips welcomed him as she felt his swollen erection fill her, thrusting effectively to her delighted surprise.

She must remember her husband was very competitive and would make sure her concentration fell on his muscled body and no others. She was soon holding on to the window sill with both hands, taking what her husband was dispensing until they both stiffened and slumped together, Gawain holding his bride up as her legs went weak.

After a few moments of retrieving their strength and straightening their clothes, Gawain complained, "Wife, you drive me to distraction with these conjectures of yours. What I came in to tell you is that I conferred with my two huntsmen and they have agreed to allow you to hunt with us if you would like to do so."

Jillian's face must have lit up at the opportunity to ride out from the bailey and have the chance to shoot her arrows again, possibly bring down a stag. Then the smile slipped as she asked, "Do you think I would be allowed to wear my regular clothes and ride astride as I am used to? I would try not to offend anyone or dishonor you, but skirts and slippers are not conducive to the hunt."

Gawain surprised her when he said, "I agree. The fluttering of skirts could upset the horses as they chase through the woods and there are too many ways to be unseated from a side mount. So, you have been on a hunt before, I take it?"

"I was lead hunter for the last four years at the castle and have killed several boars as well as Grice. Even if I say so myself, I am an excellent bowman and can get game birds easily. I once brought down two partridge with one arrow." She chuckled saying, "It was merely a happenstance, of course. They were simply positioned closely as they flew up after the hounds flushed them."

"I don't need you to prove anything to me. I wanted to get you out of the keep and see more of our lands then that damp forest where I found you. Although we may find ourselves back there since the Red deer have trails interweaving through the woods. We only try for the stags this time of year, let the hinds drop their fawns in the spring. But we need to cull the herds or they eat too much of the cattle and sheep's feed. Besides, our crofters get tired of trying to save their crops from the deer's constant foraging."

"We had the same problems. We made sure the crofters got their share of the meat since it was their crops that made our deer so large and healthy. Although we had mostly Roe which are much smaller."

"Venison is venison and a good change from lamb and mutton. Although nothing goes over better than a succulent boar and Cook does a wonderful job with the preparing of it," he told her.

"Then if we find a boar trail, we must follow it," she announced with a smile then quickly remembered her original request of him. "May I read some of these books? I find I have too much free time if I do not wish to step on the toes of the household." She did not bring up Agatha's name although Gawain probably knew who she meant.

"So, you had a governess who taught you to read and write?" he asked seemingly in no hurry now he had told her about the hunt and his physical needs were taken care of sufficiently.

"No, I had a tutor, but I refused to bother learning Latin and Greek as I thought them un-needed languages. I studied the rest of the subjects, sons would be taught although, of course, I never went to university. Even my father had his stopping points."

She laughed as she remembered the bright red color he turned when she broached the subject with him. "By then he was used to seeing me handle weapons and practice with Sir Gunn and he probably pictured me doing so in men's clothing in the university square."

"I will need to speak with you more about this 'tutor' you had. He was young and had a pleasant appearance, I assume?"

"Yes, just as all governesses are young, beautiful and voluptuous," she answered in return.

"Hmmm, point taken."

"So, I have access to your books?" she asked him again. She didn't wish to be denied access to the opportunities these books represented.

"Certainly, what is mine is yours. We will leave early in the morning for the hunt so we should be to bed early to be rested." Then he raised one eyebrow in question.

She conceded to his request. "I am willing to sleep as soon as the sun goes down. I won't be imbibing wine at dinner, though. For some reason, it seems to make my entire body ache." She returned to perusing the books once more.

Gawain scoffed as he left the room, leaving the door open as he departed.

CHAPTER SIX

Gawain and Jillian went to bed immediately after supper, but found neither were tired enough to fall asleep immediately. Instead, they took time to tire one another, finally sprawling across the sheets in utter exhaustion. Laying there the thought that entered Jillian's mind was not meant to be an intrusion between them, but Gawain seemed to take it as such.

"How will I know I'm with child?" The blurted question brought Gawain wide awake.

"When are your next courses due? Have you already missed them?" he asked not seeming sure himself.

"I have never been very, um-m-m, regular. The healer at home said it was due to my unusual activities. She did not think I should be fighting like a man and tried to dissuade me at every turn," Jillian confided.

"Then I am not sure either. Best to ask, Lady Edith. She seems to help the women with such things as well as acting as midwife."

"I will wait awhile then because that's what she will probably tell me. I will decide at another time. I am sorry to have brought it up. It will happen when it happens." She seemed to set worrying about her future motherhood aside and fell asleep.

Jillian's easy fall into slumber left Gawain thinking about his wife and how to make sure she remained at the fortress with him. When she mentioned being with child his mind raced at the possibility of what she was really asking. Trying to figure out if she meant *when could they stop making love* or *she was anxious to get it over with* or *she were excited to be carrying his child.* He realized it could be any of those and still not mean she was content to spend the following nine months at the keep let alone the rest of her life.

He enjoyed their lovemaking session in the library and enjoyed learning more about his interesting wife almost as much. He had not wished to end their friendly conversation, but knew he was already late for his meeting. He hoped they could regain that same closeness once again and he could learn more about her unusual upbringing, which made her the contradiction she was now.

A woman who met him at every turn with the same sexual need and yet wielded her sexuality like a broadsword, to her advantage. She enjoyed their joining, even initiated them. No reticent lover, she, and he liked that about her. He liked that very much.

To learn she had a tutor, a male tutor, who taught her the same as a male heir was a little strange, but she could inherit the Crawford lands and title if the King allowed. Then she would out rank him and her children would receive titles as well. His children. He must remember that no matter what the future holds for them. They were a couple, as married as if they had been standing in front of a priest.

He tried to fall asleep thinking about what their children would look like, be like. Fierce, strong, stubborn, he had no doubt. How could they escape since those traits were so prevalent from both parents? He could picture his daughters as smaller versions of their mother, chainmail and all. His sons would be even more fierce-some.

Physically strong, but strong of honor as well. He

knew Jillian had been guided by honor and loyalty when she took her father from their home. Braving a trip many others shuddered to take in a warm carriage and accompanied by a troop of servants and guards.

He knew he would not need to worry about the character of his children with Jillian. Just that if they would have children at all. Because along with her strength came unpredictability as well. His wife could wake-up one day and decide to throw the usurper out of her home and re-instate her father.

Gawain feared that Jillian coming to the forefront. He didn't wish to have to restrain his wife from leaving him, taking his possibility of children and any future his clan could have with a Macgregor as a leader. This worried him. As well as worrying how he would live if she were to go.

As often as he was making love to his wife, she would be with child soon. Then he would need to make up his mind how he was going to treat her possibly wanting to leave. He knew she was biding her time there. That she wanted a child, a male child preferably, to hold onto the Crawford title and lands. Jillian might not cut him loose completely until she knew she had a male child so possibly Gawain had more time to convince her to stay with him. He didn't have many options.

In the morning, they rose early and ate quickly to meet the others, Sir Torrey and Sir Jason, out in the stable getting the horses readied. Jillian, wearing the knit hose and leather jerkin over a long-sleeved tunic went to her Palfrey, Lancelot, and found him returned to his original healthy proportions. The gelding nosed Jillian and seemed to be glad to see her again. She patted the horse and checked the saddle and bridle before being satisfied. Sir Jason gave Jillian the bow and arrows they had confiscated on that first fateful afternoon.

"Is my broadsword here, also?" she asked.

"Yes, Madam. We had it cleaned, oiled and placed with ours in the armory," Sir Torrey told her as he finished pulling the strap that held his saddle on. They would also be taking a Rouncey as packhorse, which intimated they planned on bagging a portion of big game and not only a couple of deer.

"Don't use 'madam' with me, please. Jillian is fine." Both men looked toward their Laird for his permission and he nodded silently as he checked his horse and gear.

"Do we have extra spears? I am used to travelling with two when I go after boars. Sometimes the first thrust isn't deep enough if we are both on the ground," she told the men.

Gawain ended the conversation by saying firmly, "If we come upon a boar, one of us will be using the pikes. I don't want you placed in that sort of danger."

Jillian resented his authoritarian decree but realized he also had to protect the mother of his possible heir. She decided to be grateful for being invited along with the hunt at all. She could have found herself sitting inside and reading for days at a time. She knew she would soon become restless which would be a bad thing for everyone. Since she would then begin to wish to find a way of unseating Dennis from her father's home.

The four rode off at a brisk pace, needing to get to the areas where game would be prevalent and worth spending the time culling. Soon it seemed to Jillian they were at the same woodland where she and her father had taken refuge.

As she stood in her stirrups, she searched for any sign of her once passing that way and Gawain said, "We came out this way but you were much further north of here. This wood follows a ravine for miles so you could have remained hidden except we ran across your horses' trail and followed it to make sure no one was hiding for nefarious reasons."

"So, but for a little luck or bad luck depending on how one looks at it, my father and I could have been in England by now."

Gawain did not have time for an answer because Jason finished walking the ground and motioned them to follow him as he remounted and headed into the trees.

The hunters seemed to be following a slightly worn path through the trees. There were signs some of the evergreens had been chewed to about five feet which meant the deer had come through this way during their foraging for food.

Jillian knew the woods was too open for the deer to feel comfortable sleeping in and would be on the move the whole time. They would be looking for more ground cover and brush, plus searching for water.

The other three, of course, knew where the streams were in the forest and she followed their lead, letting them choose the paths while she kept a watch for any game that may be trying to hide from them.

Finally, the men dismounted and she did as well. Tethering the horses a distance away, they grabbed their weapons of choice. The three men selecting crossbows. Jillian took her bow and the quiver on her back and followed them as they hunched over going into some underbrush growing alongside the stream. There they found a large herd of deer drinking and munching the low branches. Each hunter selected their target and as one they let loose with their arrow and bolts while four stags went down. The rest startled then ran in several directions at once.

The huntsmen went to their respective kills and pulled out their knives and gutted the animal, using the stomach to hold the various organs that would be taken back and prepared in numerous ways. Gawain turned to help Jillian with hers only to find she was wiping off her blade and beginning to hoist the carcass onto her shoulders.

"I'll take that one, too," he told her.

She was about to argue, but then backed down. "I'll bring your bow and the stomachs. Do all of these get tied to the pack horse, then?"

"Yes. I was hoping to find some larger game, but we will need to make a special hunt for a boar. Get the dogs to flush them out. There isn't always enough undergrowth for them to hide behind in the woods."

"You don't have deer hounds? I thought I saw them near the stable before," she said as they reached the horses and she held the bridle so Gawain could tie the kills onto the back. The horse must have been used for this purpose before because it didn't flinch with the smell of blood or having the lifeless weight on his blanketed back.

"We have some trained for boars and the others are used for game birds. There are a lot of grouse, pheasant and partridge the other direction from the keep where the meadows and fields are. I'll take you another time. Early morning is always best for those before they separate and go off scavenging for food."

Jason and Torrey brought their contributions and tied them onto the pack animal, all of them happy with their hunt. Four good-sized stags were worth spending a day in the saddle. The hunt went well and Jillian proved she was as capable as the men.

There was venison that night, several dishes made up of the heart and liver, pies and broths. Jillian received praise from the other hunters. She merely smiled and nodded at their teasing, happy to be accepted in a role that was more comfortable to her than chatelaine.

She noticed Agatha was at the table eating and hadn't sent her any looks that could have been replaced by daggers. Jillian was very relaxed and content as she went to bed with her husband.

Of course, Gawain needed to congratulate her in his own way and it was a while before they went to sleep, both equally exhausted from their early rising and the exertion of the hunt. Jillian tried to remind herself to speak with Lady Edith in the morning about what she should be watchful of if she were with child.

Jillian broke her fast with several of the others living in the keep. Then went in search of Lady Edith in the buttery where she evidently spent much of her time brewing the ale and cider for the tables as well as elixirs and potions to keep the clan healthy.

She found that lady in the lower level where her medicine room was, as well as, her father who was appearing so much better she exhaled a deep breath before speaking. At dinner, the candlelight hid the fact his pupils were a normal size and the whites of his eyes were no longer yellowed. His hair was still white, but not falling out as it had been a few weeks ago. He was the father she was used to - talkative and lively.

Both of the older people welcomed her and they spoke about the supper the night before. And of their gathering herbs for the coming winter which Jillian understood her father to have been helping with. She could not ever remember her father having an interest in such things at the castle, but mayhaps having been poisoned and then saved by the healer here had him feeling grateful to Lady Edith.

Finally, her father sensed that Jillian came with a purpose and that purpose was a private matter between her and the healer. He told both women he would see them later in the day. His gaze remained on Lady Edith until she smiled and nodded that he was dismissed.

"Now, Jillian, how can I be of assistance? Are you feeling unwell?" the older lady asked almost happily but the smile left her face when Jillian shook her head.

"I, well, I was wondering how one knew when one was with child. I mean I know I haven't been here long, but it is very important that I know as soon as possible."

Lady Edith appeared concerned. "I guess it is not my business why you want to know such a thing so quickly, but a missed monthly flux, of course, is the first sign. Then you may feel tired and ill, especially in the morning, but not necessarily only then. Food tastes change and sometimes odors that never bothered you will make you run for a bucket." Lady Edith asked, "Any of those things seem familiar?"

Disappointed, Jillian shook her head again. "I guess I'm not with child, yet. Gawain will be displeased."

Lady Edith was the one to shake her head this time saying, "The Laird knows these things take time. He cannot possibly be upset so soon that you are not with child. And you, too, should not lose heart. After all, it has not been that long and it is not unusual for it to take several months even for two healthy people such as you and the Laird."

"I know, I guess, but it is just that once it happens, I have so many plans to put in place."

At Edith's worried expression, Jillian changed the subject. "Is my father fully cured? He appears almost as he did before except, he is still thin, well thinner than I remember him being."

"He will begin to gain weight back now, too. I think all the poison is washed from his body and he will continue to regain his strength. Thank be to God his mind was never affected which can be the outcome of some of those poisons fed to someone over time."

Jillian could tell the older woman was seriously relieved. "Then I will give thanks for that and ply my time before worrying over conceiving a child this soon. I will take things a day at a time. My father is the most important person to me and if you say he is regaining his health, I will take happiness from that."

Jillian went outside to the bailey to nurse her disappointment in finding she wasn't going to hold her child in nine months.

Near the stables, Jillian walked toward the dogs sleeping in the afternoon sun. The big deerhounds raised their heads and then thumped the ground with their bushy red tails, their tongues lolling out of their mouth. She bent to pet the lead hound and the rest of them, five in all, got up and surrounded her pleading for their portion of appreciation. Jillian felt herself smiling easily and talking with them until a large burly man came out who introduced himself as Mac, the stable master as well as master-of-the-hounds.

"The Laird said these dogs were trained to hunt boar and game birds?" Jillian asked the man as she calmed the dogs circling her feet, brushing up against the round-dress she was wearing.

"Aye, Madam. Ol' MacDuff here and his bitch be the best boar hounds and their three pups, not from the same litter mind you, are trained up in flushing out game birds. It takes only the two for the boar hunts. Too many dogs and they can get injured when the boar turns on them. MacDuff and his Bride keep the boar worried enough that he never sees the hunter come up on him." he explained as if to a novice.

"We had a larger pack but they were all trained for boar. I had a spaniel to help me hunt birds. I prefer the hunt of larger game, though. May I take the dogs out for birds one day this week?" she asked as if she were not the Laird's wife.

The man looked at her keenly, but knew she had gone out with the hunting group the day before. "Of course, Madam. The more mature one will keep the others in line. Just let me know when you want to go and I'll point you to the best areas to get a good chance of bringing back supper." He smiled as she told the dogs to go and lay back down as she returned to the keep, thinking she could be happy here once everyone realized she was serious about what she liked to do.

Three days later, Jillian, dressed in her male attire, went out to the stable and asked the stablemaster for the use of the dogs that morning. He had a young lad saddle her Palfrey even though she told him she would do so, but then realized these people would feel badly if they couldn't help the Laird's wife in some manner, so swallowed the objection.

Jillian rode out across the fallow fields towards the best areas pointed out for game birds. She remembered the stablemaster warned it was a little boggy and that her horse may get slowed down. That was also why it was a good chance the birds would be found there, too. The three young dogs were happy, nose to the ground and heading in the same direction as she was. Of course, they got scent of the geese that stopped overnight in the fields as well as anything that came to peck at the leftover seeds in the ploughed rows. Over all, they were well trained and kept up with her as they travelled the miles until she saw the edge of the fields and underbrush. Jillian pulled her horse up and dropped the reins knowing Lancelot would stay close and come to her whistle when she needed him.

She used the command the stablemaster taught her to direct the dogs. They were so similar to her own pack at the castle she caught on to their personalities quickly and soon she and the dogs were working well together. She sent the dogs in to flush a good-looking prospective area and knocked her arrow preparing for whatever flew-up or ran out. She had heard the call of several types of birds so prepared for either escape route.

The dogs did their job and Jillian did hers. She kept working the area as the birds dropped back to the brush a few yards from where the dogs flushed them. As she got ready, she sent the dogs into the underbrush again. There were already a dozen brace of birds hanging from her saddle, but she wanted enough to be cooked up for supper.

She made the motion and the dogs raced back. Coming around from one side forcing the birds out toward the open field when there was a thrashing through the brush.

Jillian heard the snorting and the grunting at the same time as the dogs put up a noisy cacophony of barks and woofs. They picked up the scent of the wild boar thrashing just inside the brush covering and went wild.

She tried to recall the dogs but it was too late. They followed what their parents probably had taught them and began biting at the boar's rear end, turning him and taunting him into a frenzy of fear and anger.

Trying once more to get the pups' attention, she recognized they were beyond listening to her commands. She soon realized the dogs were in trouble. The boar, having lost its fear, was planning on charging instead of running. He placed his rear to the thicket and faced the hopping, biting pups with his head lowered and tusks readied.

She heard one of the dogs whine in pain as she saw it flung by the deadly sharp teeth of the boar. She also realized her presence had not gone unnoticed and now she was the target of the boar's bad temper. Not having a chance to make it to her horse and the dogs were too untrained to know how to turn the boar away, she had to decide how to save herself.

It began running at her with his red-rimmed eyes and drooling mouth, grunting with each step he took as he raged towards her. She only had the arrows and pulled another from her quiver. Kneeling, digging the toe of her boot into the ground as best she could, Jillian held the long shaft in front of her like a pike. Her only chance at this point would be a direct hit into one of those beady eyes.

Trembling, she wasn't sure if it was her or the shaking of the earth she felt as the animal charged. Jillian stayed her ground and the boar didn't appear to change its route, coming directly for her. Taking a deep breath, she faced the charging animal holding the shaft firmly and waited. Then time ran out. The boar was right in front of her with the dogs barking and jumping, their sharp little teeth nipping at the boar's body as it lay less than a foot from her. The last of its breath expelled from its lungs and her three-foot arrow sticking out from one dead eye, blood flowing profusely.

Tears of relief rolled down her face and then she began to laugh as the dogs went wild thinking they had caught the wire-haired beast. She took a moment to stop shaking and tried to figure out how she was going to get home. One of the dogs was bleeding from his injury but it wasn't keeping him from the excitement of the kill.

Finally deciding the only way was to tie the boar to her saddle and drag it back to the keep while she carried the injured dog on her lap. It wasn't easy and she probably appeared quite a sight riding up through the gates. The guards appeared shocked seeing her covered in blood from the wounded dog. The other two with their muzzles framed in blood.

No one attempted to touch her, but several people followed the sad parade to the stable. The stablemaster came out. His face creased in worry as he saw the blood and then the dog in her arms.

"I don't know how bad he is. He may have broken ribs so I tried not to move him too much. The other two merely got blood on themselves from the dead boar."

The mention of the boar had the man now looking at the lump she was pulling behind her horse. The master of the hounds began issuing orders and reached up, taking the dog from her, carefully laying it on a bed of straw just inside the door.

"You men, help, Madam. She's tired out doing a man's job. You there, get that boar taken care of." He organized the removal of the dead birds as well then offered to help her down.

Jillian shook her head explaining, "I'm not hurt. Only a little scratched up from the brush and grasses retrieving the birds. I'll go and clean up before I scare anyone else."

There were several servants who fell back as she entered the keep, but no one said anything to her directly. Merely murmurs and scurrying as someone called for Ann and Lady Edith. Neither actually needed by Jillian, but a bath would be appreciated. She welcomed removing the smell of blood and death from her nostrils.

Ann reached the chamber door as Jillian did. The girl's eyes were round with fear and worry so that Jillian had to mention once again that none of the blood was hers. She began peeling the soggy clothes off her body when Gawain raced in, his face red from his exertion to get from somewhere deep within the keep.

"What by god's teeth were you trying to prove, Woman? I can't leave you alone on your own a moment before you are endangering yourself. I didna think you had a death wish," he said falling into the brogue in his worry and fear for her.

"Ann, go supervise a bath but do not bring it in until the Laird and I have finished speaking," Jillian had the presence of mind to say.

Then turned to her husband who was standing close but was afraid to touch her in fear he would do more injury to her wounds. His eyes searched her body not landing on any one place for long.

"I will repeat one last time - none of this is my blood. I had to carry one of the dogs back on my lap because he was injured trying to save me. I guess they all saved me because they kept that damnable boar busy enough to give me time to figure out some way of killing it." She finished taking off her clothes and wrapped herself in a nearby blanket.

This was one time her naked body did not dissuade her husband from his original task. "What were you thinking of to go boar-hunting on your own. Even men don't do that reckless of an act!"

Jillian narrowed her eyes and said slowly, "Husband. I know you have been dealt a shock and I do not know what you have been told. I was merely bird hunting with the three pups and we came upon a boar that was not happy with our intrusion. I was lucky enough to have had an arrow and the boar was unlucky enough to have charged me."

Then she gave a deep sigh admitting, "I do not know if I shoved the arrow into its eye or if the stupid beast did not realize that what I was holding would be any sort of danger to him. Either way, I stuck him through the eye and into his brain and he fell like a log in front of me - dead."

After listening to her story, Gawain wrapped his

arms around her. "You are never to leave this bailey alone again. You are to let me accompany you wherever you go and, if I cannot, one of my guards will. Do we have an understanding? You are very dear to me."

"I am not carrying your child. I spoke with Lady Edith."

"That is not why you are dear to me although that alone might make you stop and think before you put yourself in danger." He kissed the top of her head. "I'll tell Ann she can come in now. We are done talking for a while."

At supper, the talk was of naught but Jillian's besting a wild boar on her own and without weapons and then riding in like a conquering hero with the injured dog on her lap. She finally had to leave, unable to stop the comments from all around her.

Agatha watched her but didn't say anything one way or the other. Jillian was sure she thought that the wife of a Laird should not be out hunting boar like some common huntsman and should not have sunk so low as to carry a dog on her lap, wounded or not.

Gawain followed closely and said casually as he undressed, "The grouse were very tasty and the partridge pie was one of Cook's best."

Jillian accepted the compliment as she was sure he meant it. "Fresh game bird is a delight no matter how it is cooked, but you are right in that the pie was the best I have ever had, also. My father did not have much to say this evening. Did he seem tired?"

Gawain hesitated, not wanting to break this tenuous laying down of arms. "He told me he was worried about you and I told him, as your husband, I would handle things."

Jillian stopped undressing and asked, "So you're going to 'handle' me?"

Knowing this was the area he wished to stay away from, Gawain said, "I thought we already had."

Jillian appreciated his use of the term 'we' and then nodded and continued to get naked before climbing into the bed and waiting for her husband to come to her.

Gawain blew out the candle and the mattress dipped as he crawled in next to her, pulling her to him as he always did. "I don't want this to come between what we have together. I do not want to change you but you must realize you affect many people around you. Probably did even at the castle, but it did not matter since everyone thought of you as a child and that you would grow out of it. Here you are my wife and future mother of my children. If anything happened to you, it would mean a great deal to a lot of people, people you do not even know yet."

"I understand your worry and it is not as if I planned on the boar's attack. I often went hunting alone on my father's land and I had the dogs and my own horse, which is trained to come to me when called. It was a once in a lifetime event and now we are through it." Then she added, "More women die during childbirth then get gored to death. You may wish to think about that, Laird." She rolled over as he allowed a hiss of breath to escape through his gritted teeth.

CHAPTER SEVEN

Lady Edith sent for Jillian as she read in the upstairs library. Jillian had spent the last few days in the room after checking on the progress of the pup's healing and a talk with her father usually accompanied by Lady Edith in her workroom or the solar off the great hall.

Jillian approached the hall hearing Agatha's voice o-o-oh-ing and ah-h-ing over something. Entering the hall from the curved stairs, she found the tables covered with bolts of lovely colored material, lace, braided belts, and chains for wrist or neck.

Now Jillian understood Ann's speculative look and she smiled at the young girl and said, "I suppose you have something picked out for yourself for a new frock?"

Ann's eyes got large as she said, "Oh, no, Madam. I thought it time for you to select your own gowns. The travelling salesman has beads and gold banding and all sorts of lovely things."

Lady Edith added her own urging saying, "I loaned you those other items since you didn't have anything with you, but they are not of fine enough quality for the Laird's wife."

All three women's eyes focused on Jillian's reaction unsure if she cared what the Laird's wife should wear, but Jillian knew they were only trying to please her as well as the Laird so gave in. "What do you suggest, Lady Edith?"

The merchant, who had braved the inclement weather and the distance to make a sale, came forward and held out the end of a bolt of turquoise blue and paired it with a silver ribbon for trim. Then he pulled forward a bolt of green that also brought out the color of her eyes.

Jillian fingered both, liking the weight of the material and the pattern hidden in the green brocade. There was also heavier material for a velvet short gown to cover the turquoise along with braid that could be interwoven on the back to tighten it to her figure to keep her warm in the winter months.

Finally, she sat back and allowed Lady Edith and Agatha to have their say in what materials and trims should be purchased since they both seemed to know what would go well together. After all, they would be the seamstresses on the gowns, as well.

As the number of items piled up, Jillian said quietly to Agatha, "This seems like a great amount to spend on just cloth."

"This is how we have always done things. We buy now and then sew throughout the year. The Laird can easily afford what we are purchasing and I am authorized to do so," she explained as Lady Edith added some soft muslin and simple linen possibly for sheets and other household needs.

The merchant left the keep after staying overnight, and a frenzy of sewing began. Even Ann was brought in to do her fine hand-stitching to the many dresses that the others thought Jillian needed. Not that it changed anything much for Jillian who was only bothered by fittings. Since she never learned how to sew, she couldn't help with the work even if she had the inclination.

She left the others using words like 'sacque dress'

and 'round dress with trumpet sleeves' as if they were in some sort of foreign land with a foreign language. At least it made no sense to her. When they began speaking of pleats and gussets and engageantes she knew she would be best in another part of the keep. Anywhere they could not trail her for another fitting.

Jillian rode out of the keep alone once again while the gate guards watched stonily. They evidently were not told to prevent her leaving and no one mentioned her needing a guide when she had Lancelot saddled. She took only her bow and quiver and a large, empty woven sack which she hoped to have filled by the end of the day with fat fresh salmon to be salted or dried for the winter. Jillian hoped Cook knew a good fish head stew recipe, for it was a favorite of Lord Riley.

She rode directly to the stream that eventually meandered through the woods. The salmon she noticed before hid in the shade of the stones and bank blending in with the river's bottom. Trying to hide from the birds she knew thrived on the fish of the region.

Standing almost knee-deep in the cold water, she knocked an arrow and sent it flying to hit its mark barely sending a ripple of warning to the other fish resting not far away. Reaching down to the shaft of her arrow, she lifted it quickly tossing the fish up onto the bank where it flopped a couple of times before laying quietly.

She repeated the process again and again, walking stealthily through the stream, surprising the sleeping fish as she invaded their territory. Finally, out of arrows, although she could retrieve those that stayed with the salmon as she tossed their bodies, Jillian began the long trek back to where Lancelot was waiting.

Filling the sack, she placed the arrows into her quiver without losing any. She knew not to shoot a fish that was right in front of a rock where the chance of damage to the point was certain.

Jillian took her bag to Cook who became very excited having the fresh salmon to work with and handed the heavy sack to one of the other kitchen servants to scale and gut the treasure. On the way out, Jillian mentioned her father's preference for fish-head stew and Cook smiled and told her it would be added to supper's fare.

After another two-weeks, Jillian woke to feeling not quite right. Not ill but like possibly she had eaten something that did not agree with her. She sat and read in the library area after getting dressed, but skipped breaking her fast, thinking it best not to upset her stomach more than it already was.

She wouldn't follow her usual daily routine either until her stomach settled. She had been going daily to the dungeon area and lifting weighted objects to keep her muscles firm. After retrieving her broadsword, she worked out in secret since she wasn't sure how the rest of the castle's members would accept their master's wife as a warrior. She had been present so long it seemed as if everyone had forgotten how she came to be there. That she had challenged Gawain and tried to kill him as he defended himself.

Lady Edith came up to the room and entered with a cup of hot tea. "This may have you feeling better, Jillian. Your father and I missed your daily visit and then Ann said you missed breaking your fast, too."

"Oh, I don't think I should try anything right now. I'll come down for supper, I promise," she said glaring at the cup as if it were an adder.

"I think you'll find that this is what you need. Remember when I explained how you would know if you were with child or not? I think this is the first of many symptoms. Now try to drink this while it is still hot. It will settle your stomach but won't make the sickness go away completely, merely make it more manageable. You must keep eating during this time because the baby is doing a lot of growing. It will be a real little person by now and you are responsible for his or her care as the case may be."

Lady Edith continued speaking as Jillian tried recovering from the shock of finding she was going to give birth to a baby in a few months, possibly by next summer. If Lady Edith noticed the silence of the new mother-to-be, she did not say so.

"Does my father know?" Was the only thing that came to her mind to say.

"No, I think you should tell, Gawain, first and then announce it to the clan in a few days or weeks as you decide. You are so thin you will begin to show in another month so I wouldn't attempt to keep it quiet for too long. Besides, if I know, Gawain, he will want to crow like the proudest of roosters about his upcoming heir."

"Is there some way to know that it will be a son?"

"No, only a strong tradition in our family. The first is always a boy. And the percentage of males to females is skewed to the males by three to one," Lady Edith confided.

Jillian appealed to the woman who seemed more and more like a mother to her and asked worriedly, "How do I tell, Gawain? I don't know how he is going to take the news."

"You'll know when the time is right but I think he will be overjoyed. You should not worry about how he will take the news. But beware, he will wrap you in fleece, trying to protect you and his child." The other woman stood and left Jillian to think about what the news meant to her and her plans to return home to force Dennis out of her father's house.

Gawain had a surprise for Jillian that evening when he returned from his visit to a neighboring clan. He brought a priest back with him who was to perform the wedding ceremony, making everything official. Jillian wanted to put off the ceremony until spring as they had discussed when they became handfasted. Now she knew she carried his child she could not in good conscience deny his wish to marry. His child needed the protection of his name and the clan, especially if Dennis felt the child endangered his hold over the title and land that still belonged to her father.

That evening there was a celebration even though the wedding wouldn't be held until the next morning. Jillian was too nervous to eat much. Besides her stomach was acting strangely once again. She would need to get some of that tea from Lady Edith but she didn't wish to do so in the middle of the celebration. She did not usually drink tea and the change in her behavior could become fodder for the gossip mill that any castle can become when someone thinks they know something no one else does.

The priest sat next to her on the dais and was very pleasant and pleased to be able to do this favor for the Laird. Evidently the priest travelled in this area often and would make the keep one of his resting places if he would be welcomed. Jillian told the man that, of course, he would be and glanced over to her husband to see if he had over-heard and he had.

She slept alone for the first night since her handfasting, which made her a little uneasy. She was used to hearing Gawain's breathing next to her, his arm or leg thrown over her body to make sure she was where he left her. She found she missed his warmth as early morning brought the coldest air.

Ann came in early with the tub for Jillian's weekly bath and buckets of water followed. Jillian remained in bed until everything was made ready and then got out hopping into the tub before she became too chilled. She bathed and Ann came in with a dress the women had hurried to finish. Green brocade trimmed with gold and accompanied with a sheer veil held in place by a ring of gold chain. There were slippers to match, trimmed with gold colored buttons and beads.

Lord Riley came to accompany his daughter to the great hall where an altar had been improvised. She walked toward the priest and her husband, his blue eyes clear and bright with appreciation of her appearance. She left her hair down as usual but she thought it was how he liked it as well. She couldn't smile but Gawain couldn't stop so between the two the clan was happy with their performance. She said her part as Gawain said his and then they were man and wife. Never to be put asunder.

Jillian felt as if she were going through a type of dream, but answered when spoken to and must have answered appropriately because no one seemed to question her or look at her strangely.

The day was to be treated as a holiday. No one was

to work except those who cared for the animals and those who worked in the kitchen. Everyone was in a joyous mood. Some bemoaned that there was no roasted boar. They had eaten the one Jillian killed the day after she came back in that bloody state. At least the pup survived and his mother was to give birth to another litter in a few weeks.

But the kitchens did well in the short time to prepare and no one was disappointed with the feast as it arrived platter by platter and bowl by bowl.

Jillian didn't dare eat much and drank not at all. The smell of wine or cider almost turning her stomach. As she remembered the day, she was locked into the dungeon drinking so much wine, she felt she turned the same green as her dress. Soon the festivities were well on their way. She thought to escape, return to the room, and get out of her finery before she was sick all over it.

Gawain seemed worried, but she smiled and explained she had not slept the night before due to excitement. He nodded and then his attention was occupied by the musician who began playing a Scottish ballad while many joined in singing the familiar words.

Jillian just made it to her room running to the chamber pot before laying down on the bed waiting for her stomach to remain at the correct end of her throat.

Gawain found her when he came in for bed. He woke her up and then questioned why she hadn't even undressed before laying down.

"I guess I only thought I'd rest a moment and the next thing you woke me. I'll get out of this dress now, though. It really is too lovely to wrinkle." She began to untie the lacings to remove the dress. Gawain came over to help her, kissing her shoulder as it became bare to his sight.

He was removing the last piece of clothing when Jillian smelled the sickly-sweet odor of wine on his breath. Looking wide-eyed at him, she covered her mouth with one hand and ran to the chamber pot once again. She dry-heaved into the container beginning to wish she had asked for the damnable tea in front of everyone.

Gawain watched in astonishment and then demanded, "Jillian, what's wrong? You're ill and you haven't touched any food to speak of today." At her inability to answer him he continued, "I'm going to call Lady Edith to help you."

Jillian waved her hand, but he was already on his way towards the door when she called out, "Stop, she already knows."

He did stop and turned asking, "She knows what? That you're ill?"

Jillian was shaking her head but wasn't sure if he was watching her way so said out loud, "That I am with child. I will be sick for the next six weeks or so."

Gawain appeared as if he were poleaxed and went to her aid holding her shoulders and said, "Why didn't you tell me. I would have made this day less strenuous for you. Why didn't Lady Edith tell me?"

"She…" Then Jillian tried again. "She wanted me to do so at a good time. I only found out yesterday when I first began getting ill. This is not fun, Gawain. No one tells you how awful you feel carrying a baby. I simply wish to curl up and sleep," she said not caring it was, in fact, his wedding night once again. It was her wedding night too, and she wanted to sleep.

"Is there anything I can do?" When he saw the

jaundiced-eye she gave him, he couldn't help a smile slipping out as he finished, "I mean other than what I've already done?"

Jillian almost crawled to the bed "Lady Edith said you would be crowing like a cockerel over this. I just did not realize how angry that would make me."

"I'm sorry, Wife. I'll try not to 'crow' too loudly and wake you. I'll join you as soon as I get my clothes off." He covered her gently so she wasn't disturbed.

With one last warning, she said, "If you think to celebrate with me this night, beware or you may get a great deal more than you expect."

He smiled at his wife as he said a forlorn goodbye to the night of lovemaking he had planned. He undressed, blew out the candle and gently slid in next to his wife who was quietly snoring contentedly. He lay in bed listening to her breathing and marveled at how much of a change his life had made since meeting this woman and now how much it will change again when the baby came.

That thought reminded him he would need to speak with Lady Edith to ensure he did not endanger either Jillian or their unborn child with anything he did. His heart swelled imagining what it would feel like to hold a son or daughter in his arms. If reality was only a tenth of that, he would be breathless with the beauty of it.

In the morning, Jillian remained as quietly in the bed as she could. Not because she was afraid Gawain would insist on his husbandly rights, but because she didn't wish to spend time with her head over the chamber pot again.

Gawain was dressed when he came over and asked if she needed anything before he left. At her whispered denial for anything, he leaned over and kissed her forehead then ran into Ann as soon as he opened the door. The girl was standing there with a steaming cup of tea and Gawain sent her in to Jillian saying he hoped the tisane would aid Jillian's illness.

As the next few days passed, so did the worse of the sickness plaguing Jillian. She learned to drink the tea each morning and stick to porridge and bannocks for the morning meal, and simple broiled or roasted game birds and chicken for supper. Most root vegetables seemed to be acceptable to her stomach, but the odor of wine and hard cider still made her glance toward any nearby bucket.

Jillian checked with Lady Edith and found out Gawain had been there before her but the kind lady explained the same answers to the couple's worries.

"Lovemaking will not harm the baby and you can continue right up to the confinement or until it becomes uncomfortable."

The mother-to-be left thinking that although that was what she was most concerned about, how did she get over the fact they had been making love only to conceive. Now that the goal was met, how did they continue for new reasons?

Gawain was the first to break down nuzzling his wife's neck as he curled around her one morning. "You're going to think me a selfish pig, but I miss you."

When Jillian didn't say anything, he continued, "I miss our bodies being together, your little pants of breath just before you shatter around me, the way you make me feel when I've pleasured you and you pull me into you."

Jillian heard him sigh and then she felt him begin to leave the bed when she said quickly, "I miss that, too." This confession had him stopped in midmotion. She felt the cover return over him and he slid closer, letting his erection bump into her backside.

"I made sure it was safe, you know, for the baby and for you," he offered in case she was worried about the same things.

"I did too and I think I feel much better now. And I miss you, too," she confided as she turned towards him which encouraged him to initiate his lovemaking as he had done prior to her announcement she was carrying his child.

"Let me know if I'm too, too aggressive or anything," he told her but finally she took over the lead when his extra care of her was frustrating more than relieving her mind. She took the upper position which left her husband to pleasure her as she knew he had wanted to do for the past three days. They were both gentler with one another and reached the pinnacle together causing Jillian to sleep afterward more soundly than she had in a week.

Life going back to normal, with Gawain leaving her each morning and returning in the evening just before supper, left Jillian feeling more restless then before. She had read several of the books already, but needed more exercise than reading and lovemaking provided.

She continued lifting kegs in the dungeon and practicing with her blade, but it wasn't the same as having an opponent. She knew better than to approach any of Gawain's men. One day as she was visiting, Lancelot, in the stables, she noticed a lad and how he was mimicking the motions of the swordsmen practicing in the outer bailey.

She cleared her throat and brought the boy's attention to her, evidently unaware of her presence. "You are interested in learning to be a warrior? Mayhap a knight?" she asked.

The lad named, Leo, looked right at her and said plainly, "Yes, Madam. It has been my dream but everyone tells me I'm too small. That I will always be too small to fight properly." His jaw jutted out in defiance of the agreement he thought she would add to the other's view.

Instead she said, "They told me that, too. I had to work very hard to get enough strength to lift and swing a broadsword in combat. If you have the determination, then you can do it. How old are you?"

"I have fifteen years, Madam, and I'm a hard worker and am determined to become a warrior if I never make Knight."

"Then I can give you some instruction, but first you should build the strength in your arms and shoulders. Your legs too must be strong enough to hold your position while wielding a broadsword." She made the decision. "I lift kegs now, but I began with logs and kept getting bigger and bigger logs until I was strong enough to carry the broadsword and control my swings. Accuracy is a must and if you cannot wield it properly then you are a danger to yourself and the other men in your troop."

"I understand, Madam. I'm thought of as strong already by most. Probably because I lift the bags of grain and all the equipment from saddles to wagon gear. Will you truly help me learn how to be a knight?" Leo asked his eyes bright with promise.

"I will. Give yourself a few weeks of lifting weights first then I will take my broadsword with us one day. We can practice away from the fortress. Until you feel more confident, we will keep this between the two of us."

"Yes, Madam." His broad smile made her smile widely in return. "Did you want, Lancelot, saddled now? Do you need someone to ride out with you?"

Jillian had been riding every day since Lady Edith said exercise would be good for her and as long as she wasn't galloping or taking jumps. There would be no danger for Jillian to ride out in the fields close to the outer-wall.

"Yes, I'll take him out towards the woods but won't go very far. I'm sure the guards will keep me in their sight."

"Yes, Madam. I'll expect you back in two hours then. Do you wish to take the Pup with you? He'd like the run."

Jillian looked at the cage where the dogs were resting. She knew the one Pup from the others even though they were all identical to some people. They had formed a bond the day he saved her life by attacking the wild boar and she had saved his by carrying him back to the keep on her lap.

She smiled again saying, "Yes, Pup, can come along. Lancelot is used to him running beneath his feet."

Soon Jillian, horse and dog were riding out through the open gate towards the woods. As she had told Leo, she rode along the edge of the forest and kept watch for any sort of predator. Although the forest did not have the underbrush that wild boar liked, there was the chance they were hiding there or crossing through to get to better feeding areas. Pup ran ahead and returned, nose to the ground catching scent of something interesting, but soon losing attention just as young children do when another scent crossed his path.

This was the most freedom Jillian ever felt lately. Everyone was so solicitous in the house she was going mad with it. Even Agatha had done a complete reversal of opinion since it was announced Jillian would be producing the next generation. It began with Agatha greeting her with a cup of the hot tea that calmed Jillian's stomach one morning and she had been doing little things for Jillian ever since.

Jillian at first wondered if the cup had been poisoned but then realized the woman was trying to make up for her previous antagonism. It seemed that if Jillian was bearing Gawain's child then she must be planning on staying. Agatha must have then decided to accept Jillian as a family member, which brought about the new behavior.

That behavior included making baby clothes out of the linen and muslin bought from the cloth merchant. The women of the keep made their own wools, both yarns and woven goods which, she was told, would make up the rest of the baby's layette. The solicitation was about to drive her mad and these rides were what kept her from feeling too tied down.

Pup was darting in and out of the trees but never strayed far from Jillian on Lancelot. When she didn't see him for a while, she whistled as the stablemaster had shown her and one yelp was all she heard in response.

"Pup, here boy!" she called and reined in Lancelot trying to remember where she last saw the dog going into the trees. She called again and urged her horse into the woods hoping that Pup would bark again.

The dog barked twice and then nothing. Jillian was sure she knew from which direction the sound came and rode her horse on, calling as she went, hoping for Pup's repeat of his bark.

Lancelot went down, buckling at his front right knee. Jillian, unprepared for the lunge was pitched forward over the horse's head when that animal came to an abrupt stop. She lay on the damp dirt, the odor of rotting leaves and mushrooms heavy in her nostrils.

Her first thought was of how Lady Edith told her riding would not be harmful as long as she did not take a fall. And how Jillian said she had never been thrown from a horse in her life and Lancelot was not the kind to be skittish, even if he fell into a pit of adders.

Trying to tell if she were bleeding or if there were any pain in her stomach, she was relieved when she found nothing but an ache in her ankle. She would never forgive herself if her need for freedom caused injury to her unborn child.

Placing her hand over her still flat stomach, she whispered, "Stay tight little one. I'll get you home."

Lancelot was neighing and whinnying in fear as he tried to pull his leg from a hole that appeared in their path, the left knee resting against the ground as he repeatedly tried to stand using his hind legs. His cannon was scraped and the pastern bleeding slightly from a cut as he tried getting himself out of the hole. She could see the wounds as she tried to get to Lancelot's head.

Jillian stood to help then fell back, her left foot

twisted in the stirrup when Lancelot went down. Pain shot through her and she winced, crying out in distress as she toppled back to the ground. She reached for her ankle trying to ease the pain.

Using soothing tones, she calmed the horse, her voice settling him as he snorted with increased breaths. At least he stopped fighting to pull his leg out of the mud and waited, winded and sweating.

Rolling across the wet soil to her horse, she studied the hole, which did not seem to have been made by an animal. It was more of a hollow underground. The horse had broken through the thin top layer and faltered when his hoof stopped at the bottom of the pocket. Tripping him when he couldn't find his footing.

Using Lancelot as a brace, she stood and again spoke calmly to her mount. She helped the horse use his three sure feet, backing him up rather than leading him forward. She was not sure how compact the soil in front of them was and she didn't want another accident.

Finally, Lancelot was backing out towards the edge of the forest but he, too, was lame.

She settled him and then dropped to the ground worried about how she was to get home. Pup came over to her whining, knowing her actions weren't how she normally played with him. He went to Lancelot and the large horse met him nose to nose and the Pup returned to Jillian on the ground, again whining his worry.

Petting his head, she said, "I don't think I can make it anywhere, Pup, so you need to get MacDuff and Bride to find me before it gets dark and cold. Come on, you can do it boy. Go get, MacDuff." She pushed him away repeating his sire's name until the Pup jumped and barked and ran out of the trees.

Hoping the young dog wouldn't become distracted and that when he got to the keep someone would notice he was back while she and Lancelot were not. Otherwise, it would be nightfall before anyone thought about where she was. Other than Leo, no one knew where she was headed. She had gone further than she intended following Pup along in his excitement of being free of the rest of the pack.

Jillian now wished she had brought a cape or jacket of some sort. The dampness seeped through to her skin and the lack of sunlight to warm the bottom of the woods added to her discomfort.

She could tell Lancelot's leg was swollen and hoped he hadn't done any permanent damage. She used soothing words to keep the horse, which was in pain, from getting more agitated. Now all she could do was wait.

It seemed an interminable length of time. The sun was sinking and the chill turned into cold when she heard the baying of the dogs. That was followed by the racket of the pack running into the forest and the sound of horses' hooves right behind them. She was surrounded by dogs whining and licking her face, sniffing over everything before returning to lick her face again.

Jillian called out and she saw men's shapes in the gloom and knew she was in for a verbal lashing once her husband assured himself, she and their child were unhurt. But it was better than spending the night out in the cold.

The other men stayed back, letting him go to his wife sitting on the ground, her injured horse standing, favoring its front left leg a short distance away. Gawain came close and knelt down, his gaze going over her face and then the rest of her body.

"Are you hurt? Is the bairn safe?"

"We are both fine, except for my ankle which got hung up in the stirrup. I don't know what happened but Lancelot went down. We weren't going very fast at the time, just a rabbit burrow or something."

"I'll get you back home so Lady Edith can see to you. Put your arms around my neck." He stood after lifting her up in both arms letting her feet dangle. Walking her to his horse, he placed her on his saddle and turned toward the other men, all seeming rather out of place and uncomfortable.

"Someone take charge of the horse and get it back to the keep. You, others are relieved of duty and I thank you for your concern for the safety of my lady wife."

There were mumblings of good wishes for Jillian's health and then Gawain nudged his horse into motion, heading out of the forest and across the field. He lay his head close to his wife's and, not expecting an answer, asked, "How am I to protect you without making you feel a prisoner?"

Gawain thought it best not to say anything more. He was so relieved she and the child were not hurt, but he had prepared for the worse. That pain in his heart was worse than any wound he had ever suffered on the field of battle. The fear when he was told the pup that had accompanied Jillian on her ride came back alone was worse than any, he ever had for him or his men facing armed enemies.

His question to his wife was not facetious. It was the main question in his mind as soon as he saw she was alive. How did he keep her that way if she would not stay safely within the walls of the stockade? He wasn't sure his heart could take any more near-death fears for his wife. He knew it would break if anything happened to her.

Jillian didn't have an answer for him.

As they entered the bailey, it seemed as if they were greeted by every man, woman and child left there. Again, talk of her missing must have made the entire round of the keep. At least the other men in the search party kept the dogs with them or there would have been more chaos.

Instead, Leo came up to hold Gawain's horse so he could carry Jillian into the keep where Lady Edith and Lord Riley met them with worried expressions.

"I am fine, Father, really." Then to Lady Edith said quietly, "The babe seems fine, no pain no…anything. I wrenched my ankle and it will heal in a day or so. I have had such injuries before."

Lady Edith followed them into their sleeping chamber and shooed Gawain away as he hovered protectively.

"I'll make sure all is well, Gawain. Go and warm up or something. I have a calming tea coming for Jillian and she seems unharmed as she told us. Do not work yourself up now that everything is safe."

Practically pushing him out the door, that fine lady closed it in his face then turned to Jillian admonishing her, "What were you thinking to take a fall like that so soon into your pregnancy? It can jar the baby lose from the womb and it will be expelled by the body."

"I, I didn't mean to endanger my baby. I wasn't galloping or even cantering, we were going through the wooded area, no underbrush and no sign of animals when Lancelot just, I don't know, dropped through the ground. Like mayhaps through the top of a rabbit warren dug too close to the surface or something. It certainly was not a typical spot to find one. As I said, there was no cover for protection."

Jillian was contrite and had not been doing anything dangerous.

Lady Edith gave a deep sigh. "Then I hope you are right in that you did not harm the child." As an afterthought, she added, "You never lost consciousness, felt nauseous or dizzy?"

"No, it was more in slow motion. I put out my hands to catch myself as Lancelot's left leg went through and I would have been fine except my boot twisted in the stirrup. I was not set free until after I was on the ground. Lancelot took the worse of it," she explained.

"That's all and well, for Lancelot isn't carrying the Laird's child."

Ann was at the door with the hot tisane and all further admonishments and recriminations ceased. Jillian insisted everyone go down to supper and that the rest of the clan be assured she had a minor sprain, which needed rest. They were to let it be known the future heir was safe and secure, also.

Lady Edith agreed that was the best way to go on and the two of them convinced Gawain to go down to supper. That Jillian was fine and needed to keep the ankle elevated in her room.

Ann brought a meal, but Jillian didn't have much of an appetite. Now that she was assured the babe was fine, she worried about Lancelot and how his leg was. Hoping he wouldn't need to be put down if it was worse than a sprain.

The sound of her husband entering the room had her worrying more about how he was going to handle her not following his orders about having a rider go out with her when she left the bailey.

"Both you and the bairn are fine? I know I have asked but I worry you are keeping something from me so I will not get angry. Lady Edith was up here with you for quite a while."

"We are both fine, husband. There are no signs the babe did not ride out the fall in comfort. I would not hide such information from you even if I feared a beating," she tried to tease and reassure him at the same time.

He looked up at her with serious eyes and told her, "If I thought such punishment would make you hesitate to take risks, I might consider it. You keep frightening me past endurance sometimes and then I am so glad to see you still breathing, I forgive you anything."

Jillian was humbled by this man's honesty as to his weakness for her and she wanted to assure him she did not intentionally do things to endanger her life or that of their child's.

"I would never do anything to harm this child I carry and I do not do things without thinking of the consequences first. Lancelot should not have fallen at all, but it was as if the ground gave way," she tried to explain the unusual circumstance.

Gawain carried her to the bed and laid her down, undressing quickly to slide in beside her. He leaned over asking, "Are your breasts still tender?" As he kissed each one lightly on the side and slid further down her body to press kisses over her stomach where he determined the baby lay. "Is this the right place, do you think?"

Jillian's breath caught in her throat as she answered, "Y-y-yes, but I told you he's fine."

"So, you think it is a boy, too? Lady Edith has predicted it as such." He gave one last kiss there and continued down to the soft curls and positioned himself to give her pleasure.

"Gawain, you don't have to do that. I can make love as usual. Lady Edith gave me no indication she was worried about the babe," she coaxed him to return to her side.

"I want to be here. Let me do this for you." He covered the engorged bud eagerly awaiting his attentions.

After Jillian reached her peak, the inner trembling calmed and soothed, Gawain returned to her side leaving his hand over her lower stomach in protective ownership.

"We can do more if you like," she offered. "I am not opposed to giving you pleasure, husband."

"Perhaps in the morning when I'm sure you have come to no harm. I just want to lay next to you and know you are safe," he admitted setting the pattern for their intimate moments again, both evening and early morning as when they were first handfasted.

Jillian, exhausted, fell asleep right after they stopped talking. It took a little longer for Gawain to relax and feel comfortable enough to sleep.

His mind kept going back to when Leo had come running to find him when the pup came back without Jillian. That was the first he knew she had left the keep without an escort again. And once again his heart almost burst with dread as he yelled at his men to hurry with the readying of their mounts and questioning the men on the walls as to which direction she had gone when she left.

When he realized how long she had been absent, his worst fears were set loose to taunt him that she had finally left him and sent the dog home once she was far enough away. He could not divest himself of those worries until he calmed and thought more rationally. Knowing she would not leave her father, the only thing he could hold on to was that she would be found safe. Anyway, that is what he kept telling himself. Otherwise he would be tempted to lock her in a room with him being the only key holder.

That seemed desperate, even to relieve his uncertainties. He had to control his fear of losing her as well as her wanting to leave him, this home he made for her. He could not think of a safe way for Jillian to have the needed freedom without placing her and now their unborn child in danger. Why couldn't she see that as well? He had never been in so much disquiet in his life. And feeling so blessed at the same time.

The next few days, Jillian limped around the keep and rested with her foot on a pillow until the swelling went down and the purple bruise turned a brownish yellow. Ann checked on her every half hour and Lady Edith or her father, often both together, checked on her comfort each hour. Jillian was getting restless for less care and more open space.

To keep occupied, she made plans for Leo and how they could sneak away for some practice with real equipment. The other problem that kept nagging at her was how Lancelot had gotten injured. She hoped she hadn't missed seeing an animal borough, but it seemed more like the earth sank away than anything else. She had not made it all the way out to the stable on her own but Ann brought back reports from Leo so she knew Lancelot was recuperating at about the same pace she was.

CHAPTER EIGHT

Gawain was less strict about Jillian's leaving the keep as long as she was accompanied by another human. She made arrangements to take Leo with her and sometimes Pup on her outings. She used these times as training sessions for Leo and to find the spot where Lancelot had fallen.

It took several trips before she found the area in the woods where it happened. Jillian was surprised at how far she had travelled with Pup, well out of sight of the keep and the guards' view. She left Leo practicing his thrusts and back-swings to search for the hole.

Not wishing to endanger Lancelot again, she walked from the edge of the forest through the gloom and into the moist interior. Following the signs that men had been there tramping the dirt and breaking small branches, she searched the disturbed ground. Suddenly the opening was in front of her, seemingly in an otherwise safe clearing with large, mature trees surrounding the spot.

She walked to the area where it showed Lancelot's thrashing about and kneeled, feeling the soil with her bare hand. Other than where Lancelot's hoof broke through the surface, there was no sign of animal tracks going in or out. After plunging her bow in to make sure nothing alive jumped out at her, she reached into the hole.

Feeling around with her hand, she touched something metal, she was sure of it. She tried pulling on it and found it was sharp on one side so attempted to dig out the part buried deeper in the dirt. The soil felt strange, not as gritty as she would have thought.

After several minutes of pulling and digging, the item came loose enough and she pulled out an unusual dagger, wider than a dirk and less pointed. It was of very high-quality craftsmanship but bare of gems or gold. Made of steel, the blade was an extension of the grip, which was highly decorated with unfamiliar designs. Some appeared to be possibly a snake and circles like the spokes of a wheel, but not exactly. She put it in the satchel hung over her shoulder and reached blindly into the hollow again.

An hour passed quickly. She studied her other booty dug from the earth and cataloged it in her mind. After the knife, there was a man's armband of decorated copper, a ring but not a signet ring and a belt buckle. There was also a brooch with the pin still on some type of cloth, which disintegrated as she pulled it from the dirt. The rest of the pieces seemed to be aged leather scraps and a tether.

Jillian tossed the small stones she had found as not being from the stash she unearthed. She thought mayhap Lancelot had found someone's buried stolen property or property that had been buried to protect it from thieves.

Following her own path back to the sunlight, she found Lancelot grazing next to the field and rode back to where she had left Leo.

"Madam, I was worried. It has taken you so long. I felt I should ride back to the keep and tell them when I heard you returning," Leo told her accusingly. "Do not leave for such a long time or I will feel I cannot accompany you on your rides."

"I am sorry, but when we get home, I will show

you what I found in the ground. Treasure, I found treasures," she told him excitedly.

"Truly, you found things in the hole that Lancelot fell into? Really found valuables? I wasn't sure you would find the spot again." His face showed the young man's eager anticipation of seeing gold and silver coins.

"Not exactly valuable treasure, but things someone thought enough of to bury in the forest and then were unable to retrieve them. I think they must be very old. I will look them up in a book I found in the library. Possibly ask the locals if they seem familiar to them. I think they have been here eons and I wish to find the story behind them." She explained as the boy lost some of his wide-eyed excitement.

"So, no jewels or gold goblets or anything like that. Nothing from the Vikings hidden after raiding a rich church?" he asked disappointedly.

"No, but they have an interest and value to me so they are worth the time and energy it took to locate the cavity again." Then asked, "Do you still have strength left to spar with me? We can be back a little late and I need the exercise as much as you need the practice."

"Yes, that would be a good end to our day. Let me get your broadsword and we shall be ready. I promise not to be too aggressive. You have the weight around your middle that may keep you off on your footwork," he teased knowing such talk would have Jillian giving him a good workout.

As soon as they were home, Leo took her horse from her. Jillian ran upstairs to change out of her 'man' clothes as the rest of the household referred to them and washed up before donning a lovely gold dress trimmed with velvet and matching velvet short gown. Long lace cuffs hung past the tips of her fingers.

Jillian never wore a corset and was even now wondering when she would need to alter her clothing to accommodate the growing child. It was very evident she was expecting at this point and she would have to alter her life style soon. It was odd that the most accommodating clothing was her male clothes.

Jillian hurried into the library to find the book she remembered passing over as she sought reading that was more entertaining. She found it where she recalled seeing it and hoped it wasn't in a language she couldn't read.

Placing the book open on the desk, she paged through it to find drawings with some of the same characters and symbols of the items she found. She pulled her finds out of the satchel sitting on the floor next to her and set them along the top of the desk so the light from the window shown across them, clearly defining the designs and patterns.

The knife handle interested her the most and although the metal was pitted and the blade dull, she turned the flax pages trying to find something similar. To her surprise, she did find an armband with almost the exact same pattern and picked up the item. Placing it next to the one in the book, she turned it and studied the pattern all the way around. A slave bracelet from the Vikings perhaps or was it from another band of people more native to the area?

Then she saw it, the pattern and the name of the people. She had stumbled onto a buried bag of items belonging to the Picts, long gone now but once very active in Scotland and very good iron craftsmen.

Continuing to read avidly, she hoped there was mention of such knives or jewelry. This could be a lost bag from a thief who had stolen the items from a collector and therefore someone's property that should be returned.

Jillian was dragged away by Agatha when supper was called. She would need to wait for the next day because the light would not be good enough to distinguish the patterns or designs of the drawings, which were not all in actual size.

She decided not to tell anyone of her discovery until she knew what it was, she had found. She didn't wish them disappointed if they turned out to be nothing. That and she had not thought up a good story to explain how she found the items when her family thought she was riding with Leo, not digging in the woods alone.

At supper that evening, Gawain asked, "Wife, how did you spend your day?"

Trying to stick to the truth as closely as possible in case her husband was checking up on her, she answered, "I went riding but I was with Leo and we did not gallop or take any difficult terrain. Merely the usual ride across the open fields."

"You did not take a fall or trip?" he asked now holding her hand to his lips while staring into her eyes.

"N-no, why would you ask that. I'm very careful with our child," she assured him confused with his questioning.

"It is just that I noticed your clothing from today is stained with dirt and moss around the knees and shirt sleeve." Then he opened her hand fully for him to see the entire thing. "And there is soil beneath your nails, quite different from your usual clean hands."

Jillian quickly pulled her hand back, tucking in her

fingers to hide the damning evidence. Proof she had been lying to him. She glanced around to see if anyone was paying attention to them. No one seemed to be so she said under her breath, "Can we speak of this later?"

"Certainly, wife, but I will not let this matter drop. I have as much or more reason to see you safe and if Leo is too easily led astray then I will post another to safeguard you." He looked sternly at her before turning to Lord Riley to answer a question the older man put to him.

Jillian lifted her chin and thought about what explanation she could make, but then decided she had not done anything wrong or dangerous to her child. Even though Leo wasn't with her, he knew in which direction she went and would have found Lancelot standing where she left him. A simple shout would have him next to her if for some reason, she could not return to her mount.

As soon as they reached their sleeping chambers, Gawain closed the door and leaned back against it indicating it was time to talk. That she was not getting past him without the whole truth coming out.

She began undressing, taking her time to undo the side braids that Ann insisted she wear now that her hair had grown out. "I told you the truth in that I did not fall or trip or do anything to harm our child. I am very careful with myself in that way," she began.

Gawain stood and walked toward her nodding. "I believe you but I also know when I am being led a merry chase and you, my wife, have always led me on the merriest of chases."

He smiled as he helped her untie the back of her dress and then pushed it down her arms to explore the bare body it exposed.

Jillian leaned back into him, liking the attention of his lips on her skin. "I am not leading you anywhere, husband. It is you who lead me to do things I never contemplated before." She tipped her head back so her lips were right next to his. As she planned, he leaned in and kissed her, reaching around her body and covering one firm breast.

"I will not be dissuaded, wife, so tell me all." He nipped the soft skin beneath her ear.

Knowing he wasn't going to be satisfied with any more half-truths, Jillian stepped away to confront him with her dress still hanging on her protruding stomach and rounded hips. "I went back to where Lancelot fell, and I was right. He plunged through into a cavity-like area made when a leather bag or satchel, buried long ago rotted away. I found items, very old items, from a group of people called the Picts. They are very lovely, Gawain," she finished with excitement in her voice, hoping he would not tarnish this experience with a reprimand.

Gawain seemed to know how she was feeling. "I look forward to seeing these very old items in the morning. I want to see what so fascinated my wife that she forgets to wash or pick-up her soiled clothes."

Jillian gazed down saying, "I was so happy I did not find a sleeping nest of adders I became excited over these objects. They are not valuable, well not in the sense of gold and gems, but I find them beautiful and full, I don't know, full of life. Someone made these items, used them in their daily chores and then buried them. And we will never know who or why. I can conjecture, but I will never know for sure." She gazed wondrously at her husband and smiled in awe. "I find that fascinating."

Gawain whispered as he kissed down her neck, "You fascinate me, wife. Your unstoppable curiosity, your fearless following of that curiosity and your ability to let your excitement for such things encompasses me as well.

"I look forward to the morrow then, but first we have a night to get through before you can play with your new toys," he teased. "Let us see if we can find something to keep your mind and hands busy until then."

Jillian was in the library writing to one of the professors from Edenborough University who had shown an interest in the Pict items she found. He had answered a query she sent to several universities asking if what she found was of educational value to anyone else. A couple of other letters arrived, but Mr. Butler seemed the most interested and knowledgeable of the items she mentioned as having in her possession.

He wrote in return asking if it was convenient for him to come and see the collection during his term break. She was writing him in reply that he would be more than welcome, but warned of the harsh weather he may encounter to get there.

After her first discovery, Jillian spent many hours taking a pike and pushing it into the hard forest floor hunting for more buried treasure as she called it around the area where she had her accident. She shared some of the pieces with the others at the keep hoping someone there knew of more things Pict. Even the oldest residents didn't have anything to add to her knowledge so she kept searching.

She discovered an indentation that could have been the foundation of a dwelling long since dismantled and the stones reused to build someone else's home. She dug shallowly and found some old animal bones, a buried family pet probably but nothing exciting.

It appeared it may have become a dumping area for a crofter's rubbish when she went digging through pieces of broken pottery and even corks. She didn't think the Pict had cork all the way from Portugal and that's when she realized everything, she had come across had been too new. Items she was readily familiar with and could be found in any household in the area.

Disappointment followed her home that day. She was sure there must be more items on her husband's lands that could tell her more about the Pict, about how they lived and what became of them. Conjecture was constantly with her but she was a person who needed closure. Know the ending even if it wasn't a happy ever after ending. She thought that may possibly be a given since there were no longer Picts or even the memory of the people ever being here. The book she had access to was the closest information as to their lifestyle and possibly beliefs.

Arm bands and a few ideas that the Picts, at least the men, were marked with similar decorations like the Viking. But Jillian wanted to know more, know everything. Did the women leave their hair long or cut it short for convenience? Were the children watched closely or sent out to fend for themselves? Was there a central government like a king or was it more of small bands working in an area? Farmers or gatherers? Hunters or herders? How would she find the answers? And if she didn't, would the questions drive her mad?

All the possibilities as to how they came to live there. Where they came from and where they went.

Then luck was with her when she discerned a rock formation near and overlooking the stream meandering through the trees. She approached the cave-like opening thinking it could possibly be an area where the iron ore used in the items she found was once mined. Instead, she discovered a few hunting implements, a pole similar to a pike and the wood portion of a bow, and another armband hidden under the dirt blown in over the centuries.

The band was similar to the one she found earlier, but not an exact match although she recognized some of the designs as those having belonged to the Pict. She became very excited and couldn't wait to tell Leo who was waiting for her not far away. Ever since Gawain threatened to find someone more mature and probably stricter to watch over her when she left the bailey. Jillian made sure Leo was close at hand should anything befall her, like a sprained ankle again.

"Leo, come look. I found more treasure," she said teasingly knowing the boy was less than enthused with her attempts to find more of the old Pict artifacts. As he began to walk over to her, there was a thrashing through the trees and brush along the stream. Two large, burly men burst through into the bare area just below the cave opening.

"Weel take that treasure, lassie. Ye and the boy stand aside," the uglier of the two said and it was a difficult choice as to which one Jillian felt that was. Turning to his companion with a flattened nose, he said, "I told ya if'n we followed 'em enough, they'd lead us ta their treasure."

Jillian used her years of facing down combatants who were larger, stronger and surely hairier than her as she told them boldly. "The treasure is only in the eyes of the beholder. It hasn't any value to a pawnbroker so will probably not earn you enough for a half penny pie. But I enjoy collecting it for the history it tells me."

"Save yer pretty talk for others. We heard in the tavern ye and the boy have been searching day in and day out for this here treasure and we heards ye say ye just found it. Now it be ours." The two men began to climb the incline to where she and Leo stood.

Leo was carrying both swords because the hunt for Pict items always precluded their daily swordplay and he handed Jillian hers as he unsheathed his own.

"I give you fair warning that we will not give up our findings to two thugs who will discard it without regard to its historical value."

"Aww, look Maddog, the little lady and the boy want ta play knights. Well, we have no chivalry when it comes ta what we wants. So, Maddog, ye take the loon." Referring to Leo. "And I'll take the quine." Then he headed toward Jillian as she raised her sword in defense hoping Leo would use the higher ground to his benefit, as well.

The two big men rushed towards Jillian and Leo, their broadswords raised high in the air with the strength of their muscles, expecting to bring them down in an arc, severing the two slender bodies in front of them.

Instead, each swing was met with one from the two younger and supposedly weaker competitors, causing the larger men to stumble back and re-access their quarry. They glared at one another, then roared in unison. Taking the needed steps to bring them closer to Jillian and Leo while raising the swords once more threatening to bring them down with all their might. Again, Jillian and Leo used their own swords to protect themselves from the attack.

Winded with their climb and standing on the angle, the men swung wildly as Jillian told Leo to go on the offensive. They kept the two bigger and out of shape men busy protecting themselves from the onslaught of the brandishing swords being wielded by the much slighter and faster young people.

The ugliest man stumbled as he backed away from her unrelenting sword strikes. Jillian slashed into his right arm forcing him to drop his weapon and grab his wounded arm to stem the flow of blood. Leo saw Jillian cripple her opponent. That lent more speed and strength to his battle. Knocking the sword out of his adversary's hand, he too slashed his challenger's side open, blood seeping into the man's clothing and dripping when the cloth became quickly saturated.

"No more, no more!" the one named Maddog called out trying to cover his wound without much success. "Ye win, we'll leave."

Leo turned to Jillian for orders as if she were the knight to his squire and she shook her head. "No, you will not. I will take you back to the keep and you can face my husband, the Laird."

"Wait, no one said ye was the Laird's, ahh, lady. We don't want any trouble with him," said the original instigator of the attack.

"I always tell my husband the truth and he will wish to know what I did today. You must pay for your mercenary crime and Leo and I will stand witness." She picked up their adversaries' swords and took the knives off their waist belts. Searching for any others in the men's boots, the two victors marched them out to where the horses were tied near the start of the forest.

Jillian wasn't happy with this whole afternoon now she was escorting her attackers, home. Her husband would not treat her as a conquering hero but as a miscreant wife. She damned the eyes of her two prisoners and let Leo take the lead as the men tried to remain seated on their horses while tied and bleeding.

The group was met with a very angry Gawain on bareback a half-mile from the keep and Jillian put up her hand saying, "Please, not now."

Not seeing blood on his wife, but bloody wounds on the two men, he stiffened with fury. He held his tongue but he had never had to bite it so hard or for so long before. He rode his destrier next to his wife and kept glancing at her face, which was a mask. He knew he wasn't going to have a restful sleep that night.

Once though the gates all hell seemed to break lose as the wounded men were yanked roughly off their horses and Leo explained they had tried to rob Jillian and attacked them both without provocation. Gawain lifted Jillian down and held her a moment before leading her into the keep and up the stairs.

"Should we call for Edith?" he asked worried now at how quiet his wife was being.

"No, I am…we are fine, do not fret, husband," she said as she entered their chamber and began removing the soiled men's clothes she would probably never wear again. "It was not my fault. I was merely hunting for artifacts and these two men accosted us."

"And you just happened to have a broadsword at

your side? And Leo had one, too? How convenient," he said sarcastically.

"I often have my sword with me along with a bow and quiver in case we run into a wild cat or other predator. I always keep myself safe, Gawain, I really do." He saw the tears forming and knew he always weakened when faced with his wife's tears.

He pulled her body into his arms. "You know what I have to tell you and that you must obey me although I wish it were otherwise."

He watched as his wife wiped the tears from her cheeks and nodded, not arguing or stomping in frustration as he almost wished she would do instead of this quiet acceptance of his edict.

Because although he wanted to please her, to keep her content and happy, he wanted her safe the most. She had just shown him that being safe, even close to the keep, wasn't always obtainable. He would need to go against his own feelings of fairness and keep his wife inside the bailey, inside the keep if he were honest with himself. He did not wish her even within sight of any but the closest clan members. He would make sure all his men knew the rules and that anyone allowing or aiding his wife to evade or get around those rules would be facing his wrath.

There was a tap on their door and Ann asked through the wooden panel if Jillian wanted a bath brought up. Without asking her opinion, Gawain called out, "Yes, she needs a nice hot bath to ease her aching muscles."

CHAPTER NINE

Gawain entered the library asking on the spur of the moment, "Do you wish a game of chess, wife? Your father tells me you used to play with him and Sir Gunn quite often. In fact, he said you beat him so regularly he stopped playing against you to save his pride."

"That is not altogether true, but I did get good at knowing what he was going to do next and that probably took the fun out of it for him. Sir Gunn and I were never well matched although he would set the game pieces over and over anyways," she said looking up from her letter.

"Then should I get the board?" he offered. Thankful his wife wasn't complaining about having to stay inside so much lately. Jason, his most loyal lieutenant, was the only one he trusted not to fall prey to her maneuverings when outside the keep. It seemed his wife had a way of making even the most austere of his men turn to putty in her hand.

"No, thank you. I need to finish this letter and then I plan on reading a paper a professor sent me that has to do with the Picts."

"Mayhaps tomorrow then." He knew she wasn't happy with their situation and there were several more months before the baby was due. Gawain knew that even after the birth he would not be able to give her the freedom she had been used to. He worried too much when she was out of his sight, especially when she was out of his house.

Leaving his wife, he chastised himself for not making more of an effort to find a compatible occupation that didn't end with him laying with his wife. They must have something in common after all these months sharing a bed, sharing their lives.

What did other married couples do? The woman took charge of the home and the man took charge of running everything else. It was the normal division of labor and interests. It wasn't his fault Jillian never replaced Agatha as woman of the keep, wasn't his fault Jillian had no skills with a needle or interest in fashion. Why was he trying to find things to entertain her inside the keep, then? That wasn't a husband's duty.

But it was this husband's duty if he wished to make sure he had a wife in his keep, in his bed. Once the bairn was born, she might return with her father to Castle Crawford, miles away where any child they made would eventually inherit, title and all. It was a fear he knew he would face one day. Just not so soon.

Gawain would need to find something the two of them could enjoy together. After all, his father-by-marriage and Lady Edith spent almost every hour together and never seemed to run out of things to say to one another, never wished to be anywhere but at the other's side. What was their secret? How did they find the right combination between needing one another and wanting one another?

Jillian hated the expression of hurt that crossed her husband's face when she turned down his offer to play chess. She knew he was merely offering to keep her from becoming discontented. But she was discontented and playing a silly game sitting indoors wasn't going to change that.

At least Gawain had set someone else to work with Leo and hone his skills. The young man had real potential. He seemed to have grown several inches during the last six months she had known him so he wasn't going to stay small for long, merely a late bloomer, as they say.

Jillian was able to have the young man come into the keep to learn to read and write as many other squires did. She wanted Leo to have the best chance of becoming a knight as she could give him. She knew what it felt like to yearn for something so badly, yet, know it would always be out of reach.

Walking to the window, she watched the leafless trees in the distance. So much had happened in that woods. She could barely remember the girl, who had travelled with her ill father, before being found by the Laird and his hunting party. Her whole life changed in that instant and she would never know if it were for the better or not.

What would her life have been like if the hunting party had ignored the two horses' tracks and kept on after the Red deer? Would she and her father be back in their own castle and sitting in front of a warm fire talking of how the King had thrown Dennis out on his arse? Or would she be huddled in a small room in England waiting on the King's pleasure for a meeting so she and her father could beg him for the return and protection of their property.

She would never have thought she would find herself as this Laird's wife, soon to be a mother and possibility of having a step-mother. Life was unpredictable and she would see where she was a year from now.

She would need to wait until her feelings for her husband were anything more than gratefulness for rescuing her. More than an appreciation of his body and expertise in bed. She felt some unnamed emotion when she thought of her child, the child she would not have if it were not for her husband. She felt some unnamed emotion when she thought of her husband and how he showed his worry and concern for her and their unborn child. She felt some unnamed emotion when she thought of the possibility of leaving the keep and returning home, as well. She could not name that which was unknown to her or which of these emotions would end up the strongest.

Jillian spent more time studying the books on the history and people who had occupied the lands of Scotland. It wasn't as if she would ever know any more than she knew of the individual life stories of the owners of the Pict artifacts. It was all conjecture on the part of modern man to decipher the past. She turned and went back to the desk, hoping the professor would be able to make the long trip before bad weather made it impossible.

Her Father and Lady Edith announced their formal engagement, but were waiting to marry until they reached Castle Crawford so the people there could be part of the celebrations. They wanted the people who lived under the Earl of Crawford's protection to be able to participate and accept Lady Edith as their true lady.

Jillian and Gawain would probably not be present since it was to be soon after she gave birth. Lady Edith said there was no way she was leaving Jillian until she was sure the baby and mother were doing well.

Gawain took time from his workday to ride with Jillian and he watched her as if she would go into labor while Lancelot walked complacently on flat ground.

She was bundled against the harsh wind and felt stifled. He even made them dismount and rest near the stream. Jillian tried not to show her discontent since she knew he was trying to give her what she wished. It was not his fault she found it so frustrating and limiting.

As they sat, he asked, "What was your childhood like, Jillian? I mean you have given me bits and pieces, but I have difficulty seeing you pass yourself off as a boy."

She smiled remembering the expressions on the faces of her father's men when she first showed up in the outer bailey wearing boy's clothes and her hair cut so it could not fall and get in her eyes when she was in combat.

"It wasn't probably that much different from yours I presume. Sir Gunn, once he realized I was certain I wanted to become a knight or as near be, dressed me in borrowed boys' clothing and set me to it. He gave me exercises to strengthen my arms and back so I could lift the equipment and swords."

She watched as her husband skipped a stone across the quiet stream. "Then he had me practice against the other squires, not giving any concessions for my being a girl. I gave none to the boys, either. If they held back, they soon learned that it hurt to do so. I went at them as if my life were on the line and, in a way, it was. The life I wanted, anyway."

She picked up a stone and skipped it across the smooth top of the slowly moving water counting the skips and smiling contentedly when it went one hop further than her husband's.

"So, I practiced with the sawdust-stuffed dummy and I wrestled the squires and some of the men until I could get out of most of their grips even if I didn't have the strength to take them down completely. I did pretty well and, of course, I took them by surprise. I'm quicker because of my size."

Gawain smiled and nodded. "I can attest to that although you were at a disadvantage in the wood. You had been starved for weeks and tired, but I could see the fighter in you. I was about to let you go when you went on the offense so I had to protect myself."

"Are you saying you didn't try hard to take me?" Jillian asked watching him with her brows drawn together.

"No, I tried and succeeded, if you remember, but I didn't kill you once I realized you were a woman. There are much better things to do with a woman." He let a gleam of sexual interest enter his eyes even out in the cold as they were.

Jillian met her husband's gaze blandly. "I appreciate the chance to be outside, but not enough to cavort with you on the cold, hard ground in appreciation for your generosity."

"You can't blame a man for trying."

Jillian tried to get them back to the more reflective conversation and asked, "What about your childhood? Was it much like mine? Did you lose your mother when you were young, too?"

Gawain gazed out over the now fallow fields, comfortable telling her about his life before he knew her. "I was almost a grown man, already studying how to fight and protect what would one day be mine. As you've probably guessed, Torrey and Jason were always the ones paired against me. We were close even then and it has not changed. I trust them with my life and, even more telling, with yours. I know they would give their lives to save yours. Loyalty is very important to me. That and honesty. I expect honesty from all those close to me."

Jillian stood and walked toward Lancelot saying, "Don't we all. Although sometimes it seems we must hold back honesty so we do not hurt those we care about."

Gawain stepped forward to help her mount, but spent the ride back to the bailey thinking of what she told him and wondering what she was not being honest with him about. He could feel her restlessness every morning when he left her. Her want and need to have a destination of her own, to do something worthwhile with her life. He understood but he did not have an answer.

Hopefully having an infant to care for would have her relax and content within the walls of the keep. He worried that when her father left, she would be unable to settle in his home. Gawain would do anything to have her want to stay. He would allow her to continue wearing men's clothing, hunting with him and even digging in the dirt piles looking for her artifacts. If she would choose to stay at Macgregor's keep.

But he would not be able to allow her to leave him, their child needed both parents and siblings. That would be difficult if she felt she should live in the north with her father while he had to remain here leading the clan.

He could not find an answer that would give Jillian as much freedom as she feels she needs and have his wife safe and, in a place, where he needed her.

Two weeks later a single rider rode up to the barbican and asked permission to enter. Jillian was in the library, the room where she spent most of her time now, when she heard that the Professor Butler, she had been waiting for was in the inner bailey.

Jillian told Ann, "Oh, go and let the poor soul in to get warm. It isn't easy for a man his age to travel in this weather and by horse. I cannot believe he tried such a thing even if he found it faster."

Jillian knew Ann could move easier than she could, her extra forward weight making descending stairs tricky and ascending stairs a chore. She didn't like not being able to see her feet and where she was placing them.

As Jillian entered the hall, she found a tall, slender man standing in front of the large fire place, his greatcoat with several capes and tricorn hat still in place.

"Oh, Professor Butler, I am so glad you made it. May I get you some refreshments before I take you to your room to rest?" she offered as she approached him.

He turned, removing his hat at the same time and his beauty made her breath catch.

"Mrs. Macgregor," the man said with a bow. "I was glad to see the walls of your keep, I can tell you the truth, but I find that now I'm inside and warm, I'm rejuvenated and ready to work."

The man stared at Jillian and she became self-conscious of her protruding stomach and her unfashionably full breasts although his eyes were not roving in disgust or lecherously. He seemed to find her attractive and she stood a little straighter in his regard.

"You are from the colonies. I had not realized while we were writing to one another," she said trying to settle herself.

"Yes, I'm afraid I am. Does it make a difference? I am of Scottish descent and that is one reason I came to the university to study and teach. I wanted to learn more about my heritage," he replied in his charming accent.

Ann came in shyly, setting a tray on the table closest to the couple as they stared at one another. Jillian had never seen a man besides her husband who could take her breath away, but Professor Butler was a man worth looking at. If the girl's wide-eyed gaze was anything to go by, Ann seemed to agree.

"Thank you, Ann, that will be all. I will see to our guest, but if you can make sure his room is ready then I will be pleased."

Ann curtsied and went swiftly up the stairs seeking Agatha who Jillian knew had probably already seen to the room's readiness. When she left, Jillian offered her guest some hot mulled wine and sweet cakes.

She was trying to adjust her thinking of Mr. Butler from the elderly scholar to this robust and healthy specimen of adult male. She could not believe this man had nothing better to do during his term break than to visit a fortress out in the middle of nowhere without even a town close-by for entertainments.

"Mrs. Macgregor, I wish to say how appreciative I am of your offer for lodging while I visit the possible Pict sites. And for allowing me to study your finds at close proximity, of course. I really am honored you would allow me the privilege to be one of the first to see them."

Jillian felt herself blush because she didn't feel she deserved any praise for finding the items. After all, it hadn't taken any skill on her part, merely curiosity and boredom, and that is what she told him.

"It was rather an unfortunate accident when my horse stepped through the surface of the earth and disturbed an area where a Pict had buried his most valued items. You wrote that they did not have a custom of doing so normally. I have to speculate these were either stolen and hidden or placed there for safety and the owner simple died before he could return to claim them."

"I believe either one of those hypotheses could be correct or we, in the present, must either prove or disprove as we can. Either way, I am deeply appreciative for this chance to study a people who have been ignored as part of our heritage here in Scotland. Too much time is spent on the Vikings, but the Pict had much to offer also, like working with metals." He smiled again. The dimples that made one almost stare to see them appear again became permanent indentations on both sides of his lips.

Jillian tried to ignore the slight flutter in her chest saying, "Well, if you are sure you do not need to rest, we can go up to the library right now. I can show you what I have found so far and the letters from your other colleagues, who added some ideas of their own as to the items."

"Certainly, Madam, after you." He again bowed after leaving his great coat with its layers of over-capes near the fire to dry.

The enthusiastic scholars took a break a few hours later so Jillian could freshen her hair before supper. She arranged to meet her guest downstairs in the hall in half an hour. Gazing in the polished mirror in her private chamber to see her reflection, she tucked little tendrils of hair behind her ears to keep them from falling forward as they kept doing while she bent over the artifacts and papers in the library.

Taking a deep breath, she remembered the scent of her guest, probably not a very ladylike memory, especially for a married lady, but he smelled so…simply so good. Like sandalwood and pine trees and lemons.

Jillian hadn't smelled lemons since spring when she was still at Castle Crawford and their cook had used their juice to cook the ocean fish.

Shaking her head, she got herself together, giving herself a little talk about being big with child was not a guise a handsome, unmarried man like Mr. Butler would find attractive. Even if she were free to indulge, which of course she wasn't nor did she wish to be - not really. She had a husband even if he did walk around as if trying not to break eggshells or disturb her in any way.

She met her guest as he descended the stairs from his third-floor chamber and put out his arm to help Jillian down the stairs to the hall. The hall was filling as they reached it. Jillian brought Mr. Butler to the dais where Gawain was already seated along with her father and Lady Edith.

Jillian introduced her guest to each of them and Mr. Butler made the appropriate sign of respect for each. The empty chair on the left side of Jillian's was there for the professor.

When Agatha took her place at the table just in front of Jillian, she introduced Mr. Butler to the Laird's cousin and he stood until the women were seated. Then he did speak with both women as the meal continued, dividing his time between Jillian and Agatha seated at the table perpendicular to the head table.

Jillian watched as her cousin-by-marriage turned a bright pink with the attention the handsome professor was paying her. Jillian thought, this could be interesting. Agatha always seemed non-sexual, like a drone bee. No real need for a partner, having a job to do and taking pleasure in doing it well. Now here in the cousin's place is a woman appreciating a handsome male and the attention he was paying her.

That night while they were undressing for bed, Gawain looked at his wife as she allowed her dress to drop to the floor. She stepped daintily out of it, as dainty as any woman getting closer to her birthing day all the time, could.

"Your guest is very attractive if the way Cousin Agatha was blushing and responding to him is anything to go by. Do you find him as attractive? You spent a lot of time secluded in the library today and you call him by his Christian name."

Jillian stopped what she was doing and gazed at her half-naked husband saying honestly, "He cannot hold a candle to you. You took my breath away the day I met you and I haven't gotten it back fully, yet."

He moved smoothly, like a large panther towards her, smiling. "I don't know how long you've planned that last comment, but I have lost all interest in your guest and gained much more interest in you." He leaned down to cover her lips with his, pulling her into his body which was fast responding to her invitation.

"Our guest," she replied.

"What?" he responded as he continued kissing her neck and then lower to the swollen breasts that were less sensitive than they were the first few weeks of her pregnancy.

"He is our guest, not only mine. I invited him to our home to study the people that once lived on our lands." She tipped her chin up to allow him access to her neck again. "You know you have been ignoring me lately. I almost convinced myself you no longer found me attractive."

He stopped kissing her body parts and whispered, "You could not be more wrong, wife. I must hold myself back when I see you swollen with my child, knowing we created that child doing what we love doing with one another. That soon I will hold that child in my arms all because you were generous enough with your body to share it with me."

"I think you made your point by pleasuring me beyond my imagination many times. I never stood a chance against your charms," she answered in return. "But that seems a long time ago now. You used to need me morning and night. Now you hold me, but there is not as much intimacy between us."

"I want you so strongly, so badly, I fear for our child, that I may do you harm in my, umm, enthusiasm. I know what Edith has said and that you assure me I cannot hurt the babe simply enjoying you, but the fear still hovers in the back of my mind."

"Then let me be in charge. That way you will get what you want and I will control the vigorous activity you fear may harm our child," she explained stroking her hands down his arms.

"I can agree with that. It will make me know you are both safer. That I will not get carried away with passion and desire and hurt either of you." He became more energetic with his stroking and tasting.

This was exactly what Jillian had been craving. Validation she was still attractive to her husband as well as having the ability to drive him to making love by simply standing naked in his presence. She needed this and she would make sure they did not lose this need for one another. It was the one fragile string keeping them tied to one another and she wasn't as sure any longer she wished to return with her father and Lady Edith after her child is born.

She didn't know when she made the decision, but she had. She wanted to stay with her husband. A man she was more in love with than she could have ever dreamed. A man who took her breath away time and again.

She allowed Gawain to carry her to the bed and lay down beside her, letting her take the incentive of their joining as soon as she was well pleasured by his hands and mouth.

CHAPTER TEN

Jillian came down a little late for the morning meal and found Agatha entertaining Mr. Butler with tales of her travels over the countryside as a young girl when she came and stayed each summer with Gawain's parents. A servant scurried towards the kitchen to get the porridge Jillian still preferred in the morning.

Mr. Butler turned to include Jillian into the conversation but the main part of the dialog had to do with a time before Jillian was here. Jillian mentioned Old Bones, the man who worked on a croft not far away and was familiar with all the property around. He had told her he remembered a village of sorts when he was a boy that disappeared overnight.

The professor explained, "Stones were often taken from one place to build another, even reusing the timbers and any bricks or blocks of the foundation. The slate roofs were reused or burned to make lime for mortar. Sometimes, as with Jillian's find, there is only a slight indentation which tells us that once a prehistoric people lived there." Most of what he said was for Agatha's benefit. She, in turn, sat enraptured watching his lips move as if he were spouting the words directly from God.

Smiling, Jillian prayed she never had that sort of love-struck expression on her face when Gawain spoke. Agatha's face reflected every longing, hope, and lost dream the woman ever had since puberty. It was almost painful to watch and Jillian hoped Mr. Butler was used to his effect on woman and knew how to let them down easily, without making them embarrassed or bruise their hearts.

Jillian was pulled back into the conversation when she heard the excitement in the professor's voice as Agatha assured him, she knew where a mound like the one he was describing could be found.

"You're sure you can find it after all these years?" he asked and evidently realized it made Agatha seem like an ancient herself. He restated saying, "I mean, you probably haven't been there for a while and it is sometimes difficult to remember things from our childhood."

Agatha took no offense at his remarks eagerly answering, "Oh, I'm sure I can, but, if not, I know Gawain will remember. We used to play in the area. He would stand on top of the mound and claim it for king and country after fighting off the mythical invading Viking hoards." Agatha laughed remembering, but sounding like the young girl she must have been at the time.

That is when Jillian realized how pretty and young her husband's cousin actually was. Probably only a couple of years older than Jillian's two and twenty. Yet she always appeared older even though she dressed in the very latest mode and always had her hair styled attractively, even when only family were present.

"Do you think it too cold this afternoon to visit the site?" Turning to Jillian without letting his eyes drop to her protruding stomach, he said, "I am sure we can get a groom to travel with us and we won't be out for long, not this time at least. I am anxious to see if it could possibly be a burial mound." His eyes were shining and the dimples permanent dents in his cheeks.

Caught off guard, Jillian hated to see the smile

disappear off Agatha's face when Jillian admitted she could use an outing, but instead said, "I am sure someone will be free to accompany you. Mayhaps even Gawain and then you can question him about any other such places that possibly only he knows about."

As it turned out, Gawain was able to lead Agatha and the professor to the mound the two cousins played on as children. Jillian sat in the keep feeling sorry for herself because she was missing out on the fun and simply knew the three were digging up Pict relics and discovering new artifacts never seen before.

Finally, the three explorers returned to the keep, hungry, thirsty with dirty knees and bottom of skirts having their share of being dragged through moist dirt and leaves. Their gloves were also muddy, having been used to dig and pick up items on the surface of the mound.

Ann was excited to bring them refreshments while listening to the professor and Agatha talk excitedly of opening the mound to discover what was beneath. Although, if the cold keeps as it has been the ground will be frozen and any deeper digging will need to wait until spring. Even Gawain seemed excited about the project as they explained to Jillian there could be gold and jewelry set with precious stones and artifacts buried with the dead.

Lady Edith and Lord Riley joined the impromptu party and heard about the possible burial mound on the property. Robert, Mr. Butler, had now insisted everyone use his Christian name because his students used his sir name not friends. Robert told them the mound may be older than the Picts. He explained that often fertile meadows with access to water had communities made and destroyed repeatedly in the same spot, even if the original groups were nomadic in nature.

Lady Edith asked, "Are you saying there were people here, say, when Jesus was born?"

"Before that, my lady, centuries, no millenniums before Christ's birth." He looked at the awe on all their faces saying, "Remember the earth was created a great time before Christ's birth and man lived in communities since Adam and Eve were escorted out of Eden."

Everyone thought about what he said even though they had difficulty thinking of life in that sense, thousands of years rather than hundreds.

Jillian said, "I felt a connection to the Pict items I found. How can one feel connected to something that surely was here before Christ was born? It is beyond comprehension."

"I agree, Jillian, but there it is. We have proof, these people who were unknown to one another lived here in Scotland before the Vikings, before the Roman's and who knows, there may have been groups living and dying before them. That is why I find this field of study so fascinating. There may never be an end to it. No one knows how long the earth has been here. The Bible tells us that God made it, but not when."

He downed the hot mulled wine and continued as he stood, "I need to write a letter to my associates in England and brag I have stolen a march on them all. I am certain, after finding those stone slabs which were definitely man-made and put in place, that I have found a prehistoric grave site." He practically ran in his excitement to write his friends and colleagues of his lucky find.

Agatha, her cheeks still red from her ride out in the

cold or her excitement that Robert mentioned the possibility of needing to return, realized she might have another chance to make an impression on this colonist. He would need to supervise the digging-up of the mound and cataloging the artifacts he knew he would find there. Agatha excused herself to change from her riding habit, hurrying since she wanted as much time to prepare herself for supper as possible.

As the household was returning to a normal routine after the Professor's arrival, there was a cry of riders approaching and the gates, for the first time to Jillian's knowledge, closed. Men scattered, getting their armor and weapons and taking their positions along the parapets and at the tower arrow slots. All the women were told to go to the hall and wait for further instructions. Lady Edith arrived with Lord Riley and he took his daughter's hands in his for comfort.

"I am fine, Father. It can simply be a travelling band that needs water or food to get them home. A group of riders does not mean danger and I am sure Gawain and the guards will be able to handle anything easily. We are well fortified," she told him reassuringly as she tried to calm the older man.

"I know, but we have not had any unexpected visitors and these men are said to be wearing armor with chainmail. Carrying weapons and shields. A group of men needing to reach home would not approach with such disregard for etiquette."

"We will leave Gawain to do what has to be done. The visitors will soon be gone and we can go back as we were," she assured him, certain of her husband's abilities to keep the peace.

Gawain arrived in the hall and came directly to his

wife and Lord Riley then spoke quietly. "They say they are here for the Earl - you, my lord. And the Lady Jillian. They say they come from your castle and are demanding I release you to them so they can escort you to your rightful place." He looked from one to the other to read their thinking.

"Is my cousin, Dennis, among them?" asked Jillian worriedly knowing he would only want to do harm to her father if he got his hands on the older man again.

Before Gawain could answer, Lord Riley stood taller saying, "I will speak with them."

Jillian held his arm as he turned to go and Gawain said, "I'll show you the way to the parapet."

"No. I wish to meet with them out front of the gate, allow my nephew to dare to try to usurp my title and authority now I am stronger. I will not permit him to win easily," said Lord Riley firmly.

The older man straightened his lace sleeves and coat and went out through the bailey. Gawain, Jillian and Lady Edith went with him while the others watched with interest following at a distance. Gawain motioned for the gate to be raised, more of a portcullis with open space for archers to use if needed when the now unused drawbridge had been let down.

Jillian could see from her position that Dennis was leading the armed men, his personal guards on both sides of his horse while Lord Riley's guards and men flanked them. Jillian was disappointed to see her old mentor and trainer, Sir Gunn, among them.

Lord Riley took control of the conversation immediately and asked, "Nephew, how dare you come here and disturb my visit? And the rest of you? What could you be thinking to take it upon yourselves to demand my host set me free?" With that he stared directly at his knight, Sir Gunn.

Dennis spoke up loudly, "We are here to take you home where you may recuperate from your illness and so Lady Jillian and I can be wed. We will fight to save you from this man who keeps you prisoner. I note my cousin is being held as hostage inside the keep so that you will order us away."

Looking around at the men he had backing him, he continued boldly, "I refuse to allow her to be so ill used. You must come to us now so we can protect you and then we shall rescue, Lady Jillian."

At this outright lie, Jillian picked up her skirts to walk out to her father's side, but Gawain reached out and stopped her. She gazed into his eyes letting him know she had to prevent any violence from occurring and he gave an imperceptible nod. He followed her to the gate and then stopped as she went to stand beside her father.

"What is this nonsense, Dennis? I am a married woman and I shall bear my husband, Laird Gawain Macgregor, a child in the spring. My father has been staying with me under his own wishes, no one has kept him prisoner. As you can see, we are free to leave the bailey if we so desire."

Even through the small opening of the helmet it could be seen that Dennis was gnashing his teeth in frustrated anger, his face a purple hue of rage.

Then Sir Gunn spoke up, "I am sorry, my Lord Riley. We had been told you were being held here against your wishes and that Ji, that Lady Jillian, was a prisoner to keep you from risking asking for help. I can see we have been intentionally misled." He glared daggers at Dennis as he made his pronouncement.

Her father spoke to his men. "I am glad of your loyalty and admit I was not in good health when my daughter and I left Castle Crawford, but I soon recovered my strength once away from that place. I grew back my youthful vigor when we moved in here. I promise to return to you, to take up my rightful estate duties as soon as I see my grandchild born."

Lord Riley turned toward the gate and motioned with his hand. "I will have a new Lady with me as I plan on taking a second wife. She is eager to see the castle and work with my people as their healer."

Jillian was not surprised by the information, of course, but his saying it made it so much more real. Her father and Lady Edith were rarely far from one another and thought they may be sharing a bed, but did not wish to intrude on their early relationship. They were old enough to know their own minds. She was happy for them both.

Lord Riley looked directly at Sir Gunn and his own men and invited them in to eat and rest before making the journey home.

Sir Gunn declined for them all, saying, "No, my lord, I think we have intruded on you and your host for too long as it is. We shall return to Castle Crawford as soon as possible and secure it until your return. We look forward to being of service to you and your lady." Then he bowed his head and turned his horse, followed by all but the six men on horseback next to Dennis.

Lord Riley stared imperialistically at his nephew. "I will not detain you, nephew, since I know you have a long ride back to your mother's home. Please relay my best wishes for her continued good health." With that said, he put his arm out to take Jillian's as he escorted her back into the bailey.

The gates remained open, but the armed guards did not leave their posts or turn their backs on the interlopers now trying to decide if retreat was the better part of valor. Nothing would be gained with a battle, not after both Lord Riley and Jillian made it clear they were there of their own accord. Dennis' plans to become the new Earl of Crawford were completely without merit. He would never get a second chance.

Once back inside the bailey, Jillian felt her knees shaking, thankful that Dennis had not taken it into his head to run her father through simply to make a vacancy in the title's primogeniture. They all went into the great hall. Those waiting were told to go about their normal routines. Gawain was informed by the commander of the guard that the men outside the gate had turned and headed away.

Lady Edith said, "I should make us something to calm our nerves, a restorative tea perhaps?" She began moving toward the kitchen.

Lord Riley expelled a whoosh of air. "Not for me, my dear. I need a glass of good Scottish whiskey."

Gawain went to a sideboard and pulled out a jug saying, "All Scottish whiskey is good, Father. Let us drink in celebration of your announcement and then in celebration of avoiding a battle and then to your good lady and then to mine." He handed one filled glass to the older man, looked toward his wife and smiling, saluted her and Lady Edith.

That fine lady said, "Any more toasting and you both will be blootered by supper. I swear a man will find any reason to drink whiskey and it boggles the mind why since it makes their heads ache so." She continued to the kitchens for the tea.

Jillian turned to her husband. "You made that all possible. You saved my father's life for I know Dennis meant him harm, mayhap not today or tomorrow, but I know he must have been poisoned. Dennis is the only one I can think of who it would benefit in any way." Then she added, "And thank you for marrying me. My being your wife was the last nail in Dennis' coffin as far as the title was concerned. He will have no foot to stand on now, and my child will be the next heir if the King wishes to by-pass me."

Her father, sitting and relaxed spoke. "As to that, I have already sent a petition to the King to have you placed as my heir and then, of course, any children you may have in order of their birth. I think as long as I am healthy enough to argue for such, he will grant my request. After all, he forgets about us most of the time as long as the taxes are paid."

Then he smiled conspiratorially. "I had already paid the ones due at Michaelmas so I knew Dennis would make some sort of move to find me soon. The year-end taxes will be due and he did not know where the money is. I already sent it to my man of business in England to be sent on before the end of the year as usual. Dennis was probably sweating, worried about making the King angry when he was wanting a favor from him by asking for the title to be handed over to him."

"Father, you never told me any of this. I could have been more prepared to help you if I had but known," Jillian reproved him.

"Gawain and I came to a decision and then

operated as we thought best. You have had enough worry and upset. We wanted you taken care of and to concentrate on my grandchild," her father told her earnestly.

Lady Edith entered the room followed by a servant carrying a tray and the conversation turned to other events on purpose, letting the past hour become lost in more casual talk. Jillian did not participate, her mind going over all the plans and strategies she had been left out of because she was a woman. Even Lady Edith seemed to be more aware of the men's thinking and Jillian did not like being on the outside.

Lady Edith and Lord Riley returned to the herb room where they could be alone since no one went down there unless they needed a medicinal remedy. Gawain knew Agatha and the professor were mapping out the proposed dig site in the Library. Jillian said she was going to rest in her room and he glanced at his wife to see if she was giving him an invitation. It seemed she was so they both retired for the rest of the afternoon until supper.

He listened to his wife chatter about mounds and Picts and metal forges. He smiled as he shed his clothing, getting ready to take a late afternoon rest which he knew Jillian seemed to need each day. No matter how strong she wanted everyone to think her, he knew she tired easier and needed less excitement. He hoped it wasn't a mistake for him to have allowed the professor into his home.

Of course, his cousin may have a thing or two to say about that. He could not remember ever seeing Agatha so animated or looking so young although he knew her to be close to his own age. He would have thought she accepted her position as spinster but then again there wasn't a reason she should. If she found the man attractive and the man returned the regard, having his cousin leave the keep and his wife required to take over the running of the household.... There may be an answer to one of his main problems.

His wife becoming bored by not having anything to do.

Professor Butler spent most of everyday out at the 'site' of the mound and within a couple of days returned to the fortress late in the evening with exciting news. He told the family he found residue from a round-house used to make metal implements and jewelry. As he spoke, he was hardly able to keep his enthusiasm for his find under control.

As he explained where he found the new site, Gawain spoke up saying, "I thought that area was a dried-up pond. I noticed the indentation, but never would have looked at it as a historic home site as you have, Robert."

Agatha, sitting practically on his knee she was so close to the man, said, "Oh, Robert is so educated in these sorts of things. He can simply look at a place and know whether or not it could be a possible site for such findings." She stood offering to get the professor more ale.

"I'm not omnipotent, Lady Agatha, but with a little investigating I can rule out an area of having any historic importance. However, this may be the most important and largest such area to be found in Scotland. I'm waiting to hear back from my colleagues as to whether anyone has an interest in becoming a sponsor for the archeological dig."

Turning toward Gawain, added, "It will give jobs to some of your clan to dig and move items as well as the crew needing places to stay. A site such as the one I'm imagining will take years to study completely."

He finally ran out of words and ideas as the weariness set in. "I'm sorry. I became carried away with all of this. How was your day, Lady Agatha?" He gazed at that lady and made her blush and stammer.

"I have not done anything as significant as you, R-Robert. I merely take care of the house," she told him.

"And a fine job you do of it, too. But I plan on getting up early so I will bid you all good night and try to calm myself enough to sleep." He rose, took his leave of all in the hall, and went up to bed.

In the morning, Jillian came out of her bedchamber. She saw Agatha staring out the old arrow slot watching as Robert finished tying a sack onto his saddle. The expression on the other woman's face told Jillian much of what she had already guessed.

"Agatha, if there is something you want, you must go after it. Gawain will not be of any help with this matter so unless you think Lady Edith can mix up a love-potion then neither will anyone else. I do not think he's opposed to you, but he holds you in respect so you will need to make the first move."

Agatha peered at her in question and asked, "Do you think he respects me, then? Do you think he sees me as anything besides the cousin of his host?"

Jillian tipped her head as if trying to see why Agatha thought of herself as such. "I think he goes out of his way to ask you about things he didn't really need to know. And he converses with you over his interests which is what men do when they are attracted to a woman."

Agatha blushed and lowered her gaze, brushing her hands over her clean apron. "You think he is attracted to me? How do you know? I'm just so nervous being around him I feel as if I am a simpleton while he's so, so worldly and intelligent. I barely know how to read and write."

"But you do know how so that means you can send him letters when he has to go back to university. You are interested in what interests him. You are very lovely and a good housekeeper and we will miss you. But you must let him know you are interested in more than a mere acquaintanceship here. You should offer to write him, stay in contact with him. Invite him back next term break to do more exploring and let him know he means more to you than merely your cousin's guest."

"You are sure I should be so brazen? I mean to ask to write to him when he leaves? What if he says, nay? I would simply wish to melt into the stone floor if he said that," she told Jillian with fear in her eyes.

"If you do not fight for what you want, let others know your wishes, then how do you expect them to take the step forward and do the same? You like this man. You seem to like him very much, so you must find out if that regard is returned. I did not say it was easy, but only you can speak up for yourself. Fight for what you want and not what others may expect of you or what you have done in the past. Do not worry about what you think you owe the clan or Gawain. You have paid back more than you cost them. He can find someone to take your place in the keep if you end up leaving to be with the man you love. You must seek what will make you happy," Jillian urged earnestly.

Agatha turned to her and smiled, "I never thought we would become friends when you first showed up wearing men's clothing and knowing you attacked Gawain.... I thought he was all sorts of a fool to handfast you. I mean, what sort of maiden does the things you did? Rode with men and fought like a knight. But now I cannot seem to think of Gawain or this keep without you, even though you are still unconventional. I think that is exactly what fascinated Gawain about you. He never mentioned getting a wife although I suppose he would have eventually for an heir if for no other reason. But he would not have been as happy, as content, as in love with any other."

This time it was Jillian who felt surprise. "Agatha, how can you say such things? I am sure Gawain would have found a wife to love him and I am so opposite the wife a Laird should have. I do not sew well, I do not know how to cook except for meat on a spit, and I do not mind a few cobwebs amongst the furniture and tapestries. I am a terrible wife." She almost chuckled at her abysmal credentials. "I should return home with my father and live as I have always done."

Agatha looked sadly at Jillian. "I hope you reconsider your thoughts, Jillian. The people here have come to appreciate who you are. They know if the clan or this keep were to come under attack, you would not hesitate to fight for their safety. That as the mother of the Laird's children you would fight to the death to save them from harm. That you would protect and fight side by side with the Laird until neither of you could stand. That is a wife of a Laird who would truly have her clan's loyalty and I am jealous of you for that."

"I appreciate the praise, I really do and I am

humbled by the thoughts, although I worry, I will disappoint. I have always felt I should return with my father and lead his men when and if there is a need. I haven't let myself think past the time we will return home," she confessed honestly.

Agatha gave a sad smile again. "Mayhaps you should remember what you just told me about grasping your own life and love and repeat it back to yourself. If you can say you do not feel a part of this clan, a part of this land, that you do not love Gawain - then you probably should leave with your father and Lady Edith. But think hard on it before you do so. I don't wish to see you or my cousin hurt."

Jillian nodded as she turned toward the library and Agatha continued down to the hall.

CHAPTER ELEVEN

After supper one evening, while still at the table, Robert asked to speak and pulled a letter out of his waistcoat. "I have gotten some very good news. My colleague has offered to finance the excavation of the Pict site as well as the round-house."

He turned toward Gawain and continued, "That is if the Laird has no objections. It is his land and we would merely be searching for more information of the people who lived on this land prior to the Picts. It would mean a small contingency of scholars coming and camping on the site as well as paying local workers to help with the digging and excavation. All items found would be sent to the university where they would eventually be placed for public viewing, hopefully with all the information that can be gleaned from it safely written down in journals." Robert looked up from the letter asking, "Do I have your permission, Laird?"

Gawain glanced toward Jillian and answered, "You do if my lady wife could also participate. I am sure if you show her how to clean or catalog the items found, or where to seek more information and areas of interest to science, then I agree. She will be the warden for the clan's interests of the sites and negotiate any future excavations."

Robert turned to Jillian with a broad smile. "I see no problem with that. I look forward to working with Lady Jillian, but if it gets too tiring, you must let me know. We can pause our work or...."

Jillian interrupted him. "I don't foresee that problem. I can always sit and watch while others actually do the heavier work." She stopped speaking because she thought she heard her husband snort in suppressed laughter, then continued, "I eagerly await your return and will expect you to stay in the keep rather than be uncomfortable in the rain of our summers."

Gawain appeared smug as he nodded his agreement to her invitation to Robert to stay in the keep. Agatha remained silent through this whole conversation, but Jillian was hoping she would take the initiative and speak with Robert before he had to leave in the next day or two.

Later, she saw the two of them with their heads close together as if he were explaining the map lying open before them on the table. Jillian suspected the two were making plans for his return since Agatha was far more interested in the man than the map. Jillian hoped being alone in the great hall would give Agatha time to speak her mind.

Agatha feigned interest as Robert continued to pour over the old map of the Macgregor lands that ran all the way to the ocean. He seemed to be repeating himself but since she hadn't been listening, she couldn't be sure. She kept hearing what Jillian told her. To grab at life's chances, offerings that may never present themselves again, although it seemed Robert would be returning in the summer, once spring thaw was over.

"Lady Agatha, are you attending? Am I boring you or do you simply wish me and my project to Hades? I can understand if you do. People who are not interested in dead, long gone civilizations find my ranting and me boring. I have many friends who will actually turn away when they run into me on the streets for fear of becoming caught up in one of my escapades."

Agatha was embarrassed at being caught day-dreaming over what to say to keep Robert close and allowing her to write to him once he had to leave. She decided to repeat some of what Jillian had told her. Direct quotes if that was the only way she was brave enough to tell him.

"Jillian told me if I did not fight for what I want, let others know my wishes, then how do I expect them to take the step forward and do the same?"

Her words seemed to have caught his attention as he turned toward her and waited, as if holding his breath.

"I like you, Robert, so I must find out if that regard is returned. Jillian did not say it would be easy, but only I can speak up for myself, fight for what I want and not what others may expect of me or what I have done in the past."

She took in a great gulp of air. Her gaze lowered, fearful of looking at the man who had not moved since she began her speech. Slowly she raised her gaze to his face and found him smiling, his dimples framing the wide grin.

"I am… I am more than flattered, Lady Agatha. I never held much hope you would return my esteem and honor me by taking interest in me personally. I could only hope you took interest in my projects and I would be able to stay near you when I returned to work on your cousin's property. I cannot explain the feeling in my chest, the tightening around my heart, that you should speak such words to me. I am humbled and honored that you did so."

"Does that mean I have embarrassed myself

completely by being unseemly? Unladylike by pushing my feelings onto you?"

His head snapped up and he declared, "No, never think I hold you in anything less than the highest esteem. I am not worthy of a woman such as yourself. I am a lowly scholar. I will never own land or property. I live to study dead people, civilizations gone and not missed. I have nothing to offer a fine lady such as yourself. Therefore, I could never consider becoming serious about you, about us."

"Shouldn't I have something to say about whether you are worthy of me? I find you more than comely. In fact, I have been having trouble sleeping but for your fine features haunting my dreams. I feel warm thinking about you, standing as we often do together. Hoping my arm will brush against yours or my skirt touch your breeches." Putting her hands to her warm cheeks she said humiliated, "I should have stopped speaking long ago."

Robert took her two hands in his and lowered them to uncover her face for his perusal. "Do not hide your beautiful face from me, Agatha. I have become cognizant of your interest and I am more than honored. I realize I am as besotted of you as I hope you are of me. I, too, have had difficulty sleeping thinking about leaving you, possibly returning to find you gone and married to a local knight or lord. I was almost sick with the worry of it."

"There is no knight or lord who could take your place in my heart, Robert. You must believe that."

"Then I will sleep better tonight knowing." He kissed her hands, which he still held between his. "That is a lie. I will not sleep well tonight for thinking of you and thinking myself one lucky…never mind, not for your ears, my love. I may call you that, might I not?"

"Anything, Robert, anything for you. But where does this leave us?"

"Not in a good place. I must leave to finish the semester before being able to return to you. I will speak to your cousin as the highest-ranking male in your family to seek his approval of my courting you. I would ask for your hand immediately, but I fear he would turn me away. I do not wish to be denied access to you when I return in the spring."

"Gawain will not be a problem. You have already won Jillian over and he will not go against what she wishes. She has been your champion and I finally listened to her and my heart."

"Then in the morning, before I must leave, I will speak with him about this. I will tell him it was unexpected but I find I am in love with you. Will he think me crazy? Mayhaps kick me out?"

"Gawain will be more sympathetic than you may think. He and Jillian became handfasted within twenty-four hours of their meeting, and that was after she attacked him with a broadsword." Agatha explained laughing at her love's amazed expression.

"You will have to tell me that story at another time. When we have not already stayed up past the time everyone else went to bed. I hate to leave you, but I will not escort you above stairs tonight if that is all right with you. I need to stay a few moments here, mayhaps take a walk in the bailey, to relax and settle myself before trying to sleep for the night."

"Certainly, Robert. I am pleased, so pleased you have similar feelings to mine. I will see you in the morning at table, then. Good night."

"Good night, Agatha. Sleep well," he said as he went towards the large arched doors to the bailey.

CHAPTER TWELVE

Jillian prepared for bed and thought about Robert's return in the spring. She could see herself at the site as he and the other archeologists uncovered artifacts and possibly even treasure like gold or gems from the earth - her earth. She realized she had become territorial and protective of her husband's lands and his heritage, and wondered when the change came about.

When she found the first Pict items? When she was first handfasted? When she was married? Or became with child? So many momentous occasions could have tied her to the clan and to Gawain. Or was it the man himself?

He had been sensitive to her individualism from the beginning. Instead of being repelled and indignant of her wearing men's clothing and wielding a broadsword, he seemed to embrace that about her even as he tried to protect her. She realized she had never taken his acceptance as anything but her due.

Now thinking about it, she wondered why he was so worried about her from the first meeting. Bringing her father and herself to safety and helping them regain their health, then handfasting himself to her... He chanced causing a breech between himself and his clansmen by selecting an outsider for his lady wife.

Then the conversation with Agatha in which everything she had brought up with that lady in mind was turned back against herself. Forcing Jillian to question her decision to return to her father's castle when in fact she had no need to protect him any longer or to keep him company since he was returning home

169

with Lady Edith.

She needed to think why she felt returning with her father and his new wife should be an option let alone a motive. She felt as at home here in the keep, surrounded by this clan than she ever had at her father's castle where the people always thought of her father and herself as an extension of the king they hated. Their clansmen had supported the Jacobites and James and lost the rights to their lands long ago. Her father had married a woman he loved and was given the holding and the title. It would be right that it would pass back to a Scott when Jillian's child inherited it from her father.

And it was time to admit she loved her husband, probably had for months as she grew to know his honor, his chivalry, his strength, and power. All a knight should be and all she admired since she was a young girl reading the story of Camelot. Her Sir Gawain was much like that Sir Gawain and she was so very lucky he found her in that large forest on that over-cast day.

Gawain came in to find his wife still fully dressed and in contemplation. He hoped it had to do with her plans to work at the excavation site rather than plans to leave him. He knew she had been disconcerted, something momentous on her mind as she tried to come to a decision.

He watched as she let her dress slide to the floor so she could step out of it and his heart swelled with pride and love, yes, love since he had admitted he was a sorry sort of man who loved his own wife beyond reason. That any compromise of her safety had him sweating with a fear so intense he had difficulty breathing until she was within his eyesight or better, yet, within his arms.

His friends commented on his often lack of concentration when he was with them as they teased, in earnest, that he was going to lose his head worrying about a little piece of tail. His acknowledgment that he knew he wasn't fully invested in what the trio was doing only made them worry about his safety more.

"I didn't over-speak myself tonight, did I? You do wish to be a part of these explorations, don't you? Be one of the first to see the artifacts as they are unearthed?" he asked raising one eyebrow in question.

"No, you did not over-speak. I am very interested in Robert's studies. I think Agatha will be the happiest among us though when he returns." She slid into the bed in her nightwear. Gawain watched her with desire. Feeling the need for her tighten his groin.

Watching his wife closely, he continued, "Robert has asked if he could court Agatha and she was watching from the edge of the stairway so nervously I took sympathy upon them. I told them both they were old enough to do as they wished with my blessing. Robert about fainted with his own thoughts and Agatha bloomed, she made me think of a spring blossom bursting through the half-frozen ground."

"I think they will find themselves bound together in the near future. She has been mooning over him and he has been edging around her whenever they were in the same room. I am glad I told her to grab for her happiness, to leave us if she needed to and not feel guilty for choosing love over all else."

Gawain was about to blow out the candles, but stopped and glanced over at his wife. "Is that what you plan on doing? Grabbing for what you want?"

"I promised to have your child here in the keep and I promised you will never be denied access to him. I won't renege on my promises."

"But that isn't telling me if you plan on staying here, with me, after the bairn comes. And I do not mean for just the first few months but forever, as my lady wife, as the mother of all my children?" he asked openly for the first time. He had always accepted her vow of staying to give birth to their child in the keep under Lady Edith's care.

"Do you wish me to stay?" she asked bluntly trying to force him into acknowledging something, anything that could allay her fears about his feelings for her.

"I worry every day that you may leave me and I would deserve it. I gave you no choice when we handfasted. That was selfish of me even though I still believe it was the best thing to do to protect you and your father. I did not want to make you a prisoner yet I feared your leaving me. It is not rational, I know, but I don't know how I would go on without you. I think I would follow wherever you went. I am that sick in love with you."

Jillian's heart beat stronger and the baby inside her rolled and kicked with her emotional upheaval. She watched him approach the bed, naked and strong and, oh so, desirable. "Are you telling me that I have power over you?"

"You have always had me in your power, my love, and I'm tired of fighting it, tired of hoping you would come to care for me, tired of fearing that you will leave me. I accept that you rule over my life and my heart and I pray you are merciful."

Jillian raised the covering to invite him in next to

her warm body and he didn't hesitate to accept her welcome snuggling her close to his body. "I have spent much time thinking I was needed at Castle Crawford, that my father needed me. But in reality, I thought I would always be there. I never thought there was going to be more for me."

She felt Gawain kiss her forehead and sigh with contentment.

"I have my wicked cousin to thank for driving me from my home and for my finding love here with you. I never plan to leave here, at least not without you by my side. And then only to hurry home to our family and clan. I love you and although I do not know when it happened, it cannot be denied."

Their child kicked wildly as it felt his father's pressure against his protective home.

Gawain appeared awed and amazed as he felt the life, he created show his displeasure of being confined. He said quietly, "I will remember this night for the rest of my life. The night I could lay my fears down and accept my good blessing of having you for a wife and mother to my children."

"I will remember this night for the rest of my life. The night I realized I had everything I ever wanted, but was too naive to realize my luck of wandering into a particular Laird's lands."

"And his heart, my love, and his heart." Gawain said as he pulled her close to kiss her once again.

A word about the author...

A voracious reader her whole life, author Susan Payne loved the written word. When reading more than fifty books per month wasn't enough, she decided to allow her mind to take flight and write all the many stories that kept intruding into her life. She blended her love of history and her love of words to create over eighty stories. All historical and centering on a couple finding love and a happy ever after together.

You may contact Susan at:
http://www.authorsusanpayne.com or
authorspayne@gmail.com

Thank you for purchasing
this publication of The Wild Rose Press, Inc.

For questions or more information
contact us at
info@thewildrosepress.com.

The Wild Rose Press, Inc.
www.thewildrosepress.com